The high-pitched sound of a match striking made her freeze. A small flame caught her in the act of trying to clobber the stranger with the upraised book.

"*Building Basic Grammar Skills,*" he read aloud. A teasing smile played on his lips. "I'm a firm believer in the power of education, ma'am, but I hardly think of it as a weapon."

"Stand back," she commanded, despite the quiver in her voice. "Or I'll…"

"What? Split my infinitive? Wrestle me to the ground and make me diagram a sentence?" He shook the match to extinguish the flame, and his deep chuckle rumbled through the darkness. "I suspected you were a bit loco when you wanted to hire me to help fix up a dude ranch, but this welcome exceeds even my expectations, Mrs. Jackson."

"You're Clint Cooper." A flush of embarrassment spread across her cheeks.

"Yes, ma'am."

Palisades.
Pure Romance.

FICTION THAT FEATURES CREDIBLE CHARACTERS AND

ENTERTAINING PLOT LINES, WHILE CONTINUING TO UPHOLD

STRONG CHRISTIAN VALUES. FROM HIGH ADVENTURE

TO TENDER STORIES OF THE HEART, EACH PALISADES

ROMANCE IS AN UNDILUTED STORY OF LOVE,

FROM BEGINNING TO END!

Annie Jones

FATHER by FAITH

PALISADES

FATHER BY FAITH
published by ® Palisades
a division of Multnomah Publishers, Inc.

© 1997 by Luanne Jones

Published in association with the literary agency of
Writer's House, Inc., 21 W. 26th Street, New York, NY 10016

International Standard Book Number: 1-57673-117-0

Cover design by Brenda McGee
Cover illustration by Paul Bachem

Printed in the United States of America

Scripture quotations are from: *The Holy Bible: New International Version* (NIV)
© 1973, 1978, 1984 by the International Bible Society.
Used by permission of Zondervan Publishers.

For information:
MULTNOMAH PUBLISHERS, INC.
POST OFFICE BOX 1720
SISTERS, OREGON 97759

Library of Congress Cataloging-in-Publication Data
Jones, Annie.
   Father by faith/by Annie Jones.
      p.cm.
   ISBN 1-57673-117-0 (alk. paper)
   I. Title.
   PS3560.045744F37   1997
   813'.54--dc21   97-15898
                                                               CIP

97 98 99 00 01 02 03 04 — 10 9 8 7 6 5 4 3 2 1

No matter how tall you grow,
you always look up to your father.
This book is dedicated with love to the man
Justin, Greg, and Amygrace
will always look up to:
Jeff Davis.

And to
Heather Davis for her support of the work of
Preston Ranch Ministries
P.O. Box 44
Roggen, CO 80652
"A permanent refuge for children who have been abused or
abandoned."

*Let us acknowledge the L*ORD*;*
let us press on to acknowledge him.
As surely as the sun rises,
he will appear;
he will come to us like the winter rains,
like the spring rains that water the earth.

HOSEA 6:3

Chapter
ONE

Mommy?"

Alex's small voice roused Nina Jackson from a restless dream. Rubbing her bleary eyes, she asked, "What is it, honey?"

"The thunder woke me up," he said, his wide eyes inches from hers.

As if on cue, a swell of driving rain pounded the window beside her bed. Lightning lit the sky, throwing a checkered shadow from the sheer curtains across the fluffy white comforter. Thunder rattled through the quiet as if a freight train were passing just outside the window.

In the flash of light, Alex's huge blue eyes grew enormous. "And I just remembered we forgot to say my prayers tonight."

"I thought you wanted to say them by yourself, now that you're a big seven-year-old and all." She let a sleepy smile escape. "Maybe there was another reason you came in here?"

"I'm not scared, Mommy, if that's what you think. But since this is our first night in our new place, I thought you might need some company."

Nina tried not to chuckle at her little boy's brave tone. "It is hard to sleep in a new place, isn't it?"

"Especially one as big as this." Alex's blond hair, the same pale shade and only a little shorter than her own chin-length cut, shone as another bolt of lightning flashed.

Nina sat up and tucked the hem of her long flannel nightie around her bent knees. The soft fabric kept the warmth of her body in as she wriggled her toes on the crisp cotton sheet.

"Pretty soon this place will be full of people," she reminded her small son. "First the foreman will get here, then some of the college kids I hired today will start manning the front desk around the clock. And in six weeks, our own little dude ranch will be brimming with guests."

That's what she hoped, at least; what she'd dreamed when she pulled herself out of the secretarial pool at the prestigious Kansas City law firm and jumped into the dude ranch business with both feet. Although it had first been her husband's dream, once she'd settled his estate and considered her financial situation, she saw the advantages to the plan Wayne had talked about for the last full year of his life.

With a weak heart and poor health, Wayne had lived a sheltered childhood, his gentle but anxious parents doting on him and hovering over his every breath. Despite his love for his parents, he longed to break away. Nina remembered his excitement as he told her about the place he'd found where he could do just that, a place where he could rebuild his health and Alex would have plenty of room to play.

After visiting it twice on business, the Lazy H Dude Ranch had become like a paradise for Wayne. His descriptions and the groundwork he had laid toward buying the Colorado property inspired Nina. And when she began to worry that her in-laws were transferring their demanding affection to Alex, the decision was made. Although she hadn't seen the ranch, she trusted the beautiful brochures and Wayne's judgment, and she followed through on his dream.

But when she'd driven up to the dilapidated, sprawling ranch yesterday, those dreams had dulled. When the recuperating rodeo cowboy she'd hired to help her whip the place into shape was not waiting for her; when it had taken three hours to dust the huge wagon-wheel chandelier and sweep cobwebs from the rough paneled walls of the lobby; when she'd spent the entire afternoon interviewing applicants, mostly enthusiastic and inexperienced students from the local community college; and, after she'd finally fallen into bed, exhausted, when she'd had to get up twice to find buckets to catch the rainwater dripping from the leaking roof, the dream became a nightmare.

She let out a weary sigh.

"Maybe if we said our prayers together…" Alex suggested.

What great comfort that tiny voice, that tender heart, had been in the more than three years since her husband had died. And what a tremendous source of wisdom. Nina wasn't too modest to admit that her son was terribly precocious.

"Yes, Alex, I think that would be a good idea." She slid quietly from the bed and knelt beside her son.

"Dear Lord," she whispered, "thank you for all you have given us—our home, our health, and each other."

"God bless Mommy, and Grammie, and Paw-paw Jackson," Alex chimed in. "And my new pony, Plinkey."

Nina bit her lip at the mention of the ornery Shetland that had been so kindly thrown into the deal when she had bought the dude ranch sight unseen. The mangy brown pony took an instant dislike to everyone except Alex, whom, it seemed, he was going to obey and protect like a vigilant watchdog.

"And God bless Mr. Cooper, the man who is coming to help us," Alex continued. "Because Mommy says we can't make it without his exper-exper-…"

"Expertise," Nina whispered.

"Expertise," Alex repeated. "Hurry him here, please."

Nina shifted her knees on the hard floor and wrapped up the prayer. "And bless our business and help to make it prosper, and always be with us. Amen."

"And, if it's not too much trouble, God," Alex said quickly, "please find us another daddy to help Mommy fix the roof and to teach me how to take care of Plinkey and stuff like that."

A knot twisted in Nina's stomach and hot tears rimmed her eyes. She had opened her mouth to try to say something to Alex about his touching request when another flash of lightning brightened the sky, followed by low, rolling thunder.

"Maybe I should sleep with you tonight, Mommy, in case you get afraid of the storm," Alex said in a rush of words.

Nina tossed back the covers and laughed. "Okay, honey, get in. But I'm warning you, this isn't going to become a habit."

"I know, Mommy." Alex, who was small for his age, climbed into the high four-poster bed and Nina followed.

The bed was cozy. Even though the days were getting warmer, April nights could still be bitterly cold in Colorado. She arranged the covers over them both, then pulled her son close to steal a quick kiss on the cheek.

"Alex," she said with true alarm. "What's wrong?"

"Nothin', Mom." He squirmed away.

She brushed her hand over the cheek she had just kissed, then through his straight blond hair. "Nothing? You're cold as ice. And your hair is damp."

"I'm fine, Mom."

"I'll be the judge of that." She reached out a hand to turn on the lamp on the bedside table. A twist of the switch and a quiet click told her the light was on, yet the room remained pitch black.

Pitch black? No green glow from her digital clock radio? No

white beam streaming in her window from the huge security light outside the ranch house? She sat up, holding Alex in her lap.

The roar of thunder welcomed her. Alex turned his head and fisted his small hand on the bunched fabric of her pushed up sleeve.

"Look, honey, the electricity is out. Mama has to go find a candle or a flashlight. Do you want to stay here or go with me?"

"Go with."

The tremble in his voice tugged at Nina's maternal instincts, making her wish she could shelter her son from hurt and fear forever. After all he had been through, losing his father and having his mother at odds with his grandparents time and time again, Alex was very much a little boy who craved security.

"Okay," she said in a firm but cheery voice. "Let's go to the lobby; there's bound to be something for an emergency there."

She tugged a worn terry-cloth robe over her nightgown, then moved through their small suite of rooms and into the main lobby with Alex's hand tucked into hers. One wall of the room was a set of double doors and large paned-glass windows, looking out on the ranch's namesake, Jackson's Butte. The storm outside provided enough illumination for her to edge toward the big front desk without stubbing her bare toes. Behind the massive counter, she began to rummage through drawers for some source of light, while Alex hunched on the floor with his arms wrapped around his knees.

Relentless thunder and lightning undermined her search, distracting her with thoughts of old black-and-white horror movies. All they needed now was some dark, mysterious stranger to show up.

She pushed the thought aside and bent down to reach the lowest drawer, yanking on the handle with a shaking hand.

Wood squawked against wood.

She pulled harder.

The jammed drawer gave way with a screech, then came crashing to the floor.

Alex yelped. "Mama, mama! There's someone in the house!"

"Nonsense, honey," she said through teeth clenched to ensure they wouldn't chatter. She drew in a breath and held it, willing herself to calm down. "There's no one here but us."

"Someone is here," he insisted. "I heard them."

"That was me dropping the drawer," she said in her most sensible tone. "But if it will make you feel better, I'll look around the room." Chiding herself for the icy trickle down her spine as she slowly got to her feet, she lifted her gaze to the shadowy room. "Nobody is here."

She glanced down. The sight of Alex huddled close to her feet made her long to bundle him into her arms and hug him tight. She was bending down to do just that when lightning coursed across the sky again.

The front doors blew open.

Nina jumped.

Rain swept inside, spattering against the tile floor. Her heart hammered in her ears. Thunder roared overhead. Goose bumps lifted on her exposed arms. A second bolt of lightning exploded beyond the open doors. In that second of brilliance, a dark figure filled the doorway.

Nina gasped.

The room went dark again. Had she imagined it? Perhaps Clint Cooper had shown up after all, she told herself. She drew a deep breath to call out to him but the banging of the open door stopped her.

She'd locked that door. She was sure of it. Just as she was sure that Clint Cooper would have knocked or called for her to let him in—not broken into her home.

Panic seized her. Suddenly, she wished she were back in her

cramped apartment in the good old crime-ridden city. Or, on second thought, that this legendary character, Clint Cooper, were here. A man like that—with his long history as a champion rodeo cowboy—would surely charge to their rescue.

A low, muttered sound in a deep masculine voice a few feet away dispelled the fantasy. She inhaled the rich scent of rain and something remarkably like wet dog, then held her breath. Narrowing her eyes, she could just make out the form of someone standing inside the doorway. For Alex's sake, she had to act. If there was going to be any rescuing done tonight, she realized, she'd have to do it herself.

Sweeping her arm over the counter, Nina grabbed the first heavy thing she could find. A book. The cumbersome volume must have been left by one of the college students she'd interviewed earlier. Not much of a defense, but maybe she could use it to bean the intruder on the head.

The lurking figure moved his hand nearer his hip.

Could he be drawing a gun or a knife? She couldn't wait to find out. She had to do something now.

"Hold it right there." She hoisted the heavy book high above her head. "I have a weapon and I know how to use it."

A quick scratching sound answered her. For a brief instant, the glow of a lighted match revealed one side of a man's face.

Alex clutched at her legs.

Nina screeched.

The tiny flame flipped in the air, then tumbled downward to a gruff succession of unfinished phrases—each suggesting a creative expletive interrupted.

If she hoped to catch the intruder off guard, this was her chance. She slipped away from Alex's grasp and rushed forward, clasping the book with both hands.

She felt the man's presence first. A wave of damp heat moved outward from his large body. Again, lightning illuminated the room and she could see that his head was bent forward. Sinking her teeth into her lower lip, she raised the book up high.

Just then, the high-pitched sound of a second match striking made her freeze. A small flame caught her in the act of trying to clobber the stranger with the upraised book.

"*Building Basic Grammar Skills,*" he read aloud. A teasing smile played on his lips. "I'm a firm believer in the power of education, ma'am, but I hardly think of it as a weapon."

"Stand back," she commanded, despite the quiver in her voice. "Or I'll…"

"What? Split my infinitive? Wrestle me to the ground and make me diagram a sentence?" He shook the match to extinguish the flame, and his deep chuckle rumbled through the darkness. "I suspected you were a bit loco when you wanted to hire me to help fix up a dude ranch, but this welcome exceeds even my expectations, Mrs. Jackson."

"You're Clint Cooper," she muttered, feeling a flush of embarrassment spread across her cheeks.

"Yes, ma'am." The way he said it sounded as if he didn't realize she'd ever doubted his identity.

Relief washed over her. She lowered the book and hugged it to her chest. A twitching of the fabric against her leg made her glance down to find Alex trying to sneak a peek at the man from behind her.

Lightning flashed through the open door. Alex ducked and skittered back to the safety of the front desk. Another bolt tore across the horizon at Cooper's back, and Nina watched, frozen in place, as he turned to close the banging door. The room once again became nearly black.

"Why on earth didn't you just knock?" she demanded, feeling a little foolish chastising the darkness. "You scared the stuffing out of us, breaking in like that."

"I didn't break in," he said in a low, almost indignant tone.

"The door was open."

"That's impossible. I locked it myself."

"Well, maybe your lock is broken. Or maybe you've got spooks. All I know is, I found the door open and came in. I'm clear on everything up until that point."

She heard his boots scuffing over the floor toward her. Instinctively, she stepped back until she could slip behind the desk again.

His footsteps stilled. "It's after I walked in the door that things got a little weird."

Nina gripped the edges of the book pressed over her chest. She half expected to hear her heart thumping against the hard-cover volume. She wished she could see the man's face. The brief glimpse she'd gotten of glittering eyes and a teasing smile only added to the mystery of Clint Cooper. "I apologize for the unconventional welcome, Mr. Cooper. But the storm seems to have knocked the lights out. I came to look for some kind of emergency kit but couldn't find candles or even a flashlight. I guess I was a little on edge."

"A little?" He choked on a laugh. "I accept your apology, ma'am. The storm held me up, too. I should have realized it was too late to come on in, but I was tired and this bum leg of mine is aching. I really wanted to get settled in tonight."

"I understand. I only wish I could offer some light."

"Mama?"

"Shh, Alex."

"Sounds like you do have spooks," Clint said softly.

"That's just my son, Alex. I'd introduce you, but there wouldn't be much point since you can't see one another."

"Doesn't this place have a generator for when the power goes out?"

"I don't know."

"I'll make a note to check on that tomorrow."

His take-charge attitude eased some of Nina's apprehensions. "Thank you, Mr. Cooper. But that won't help me show you to your room tonight."

"Mama!" Alex's voice had a petulant tone.

"I said hush," she whispered a bit too harshly.

"But I have to tell you something." He reached up and tugged at her sleeve.

His cool fingers against her arm made her flinch and she snapped, "Not now."

"Let the boy speak." From anyone else it would have sounded like meddling. But the voice in the darkness had a quiet strength of purpose to it that both soothed her ravaged nerves and encouraged her to let Alex have his say. "What is it, son?" he asked.

"I found a lantern under the counter." A quiet clatter underscored his revelation.

"Oh," Nina said weakly. What an outstanding impression she must be making on Clint Cooper. She took the lantern and set it on the front desk. Now more than ever he'd think she was—how did he put it?—loco.

She reached to remove the chimney from the camp lantern, but instead of cool glass, her palm met warm flesh. The touch burned as hot as any flame on her skin. With a gasp, she jerked her hand away.

"Sorry, ma'am. I just thought I'd light the lantern for you," Clint said softly.

Nina skimmed her fingertips over her lips as though they'd actually been singed.

Clint struck a match and the smell of sulfur stung her nose. Deftly, he adjusted the wick until the lantern cast a golden halo of light around them.

For the first time, she truly saw his face. His skin was tanned and smooth as leather across the brow and cheeks, and deep creases accented his thin mouth and splayed out from his unblinking eyes. It was the glow of the lamplight, she told herself, that put that amber-colored glint in his brown eyes.

Then he smiled at her.

Her heart stopped.

She couldn't breathe. The conscious part of her mind turned to mush while the rest of her brain merrily sent out all kinds of giddy messages.

"There now." He raised a hand to his cowboy hat and tugged at the brim just enough to pass for the traditional cowboy greeting. "Isn't that better?"

"Better?" For whom, she wondered. She liked it better when he'd simply been an ominous figure skulking in the doorway. Now that she could see he was a flesh-and-blood man with sun-burnished brown hair curling attractively over the collar of his denim shirt, she most certainly didn't feel better about sharing her home with him. "Wh-why is this better?"

"Because now you can show me to my room."

His room. The words buzzed in the electric air. She stood perfectly still, blinking at him.

"I can show you, mister," Alex chirped, standing on tiptoe to peer over the front desk.

"Would you be Alex?" Clint asked, his smile infused with kindness.

"Yep." Her son strained to extend one hand over the counter.

Clint took the boy's tiny hand in his large one and gave it a firm shake.

Nina's admiration for the man grew tenfold.

"Nice to meet you, Alex. I'm Clint."

"This is my mom, Nina." Alex slid his hand free of Clint's and grabbed Nina's. Before she could react, the child placed her hand in Clint's open palm.

21

"Nice to meet you, too—" Clint folded her hand into his and held it for a moment before adding in a low whisper, "Nina."

A slow, almost liquid warmth spread up her arm, easing through her chest and practically oozing like honey through her limbs. Her dumbfounded gaze fell to their hands. She could only hope the lantern didn't give off enough light for him to see the blush she felt scorching her cheeks.

"I can show you to the bedroom now," Alex offered, breaking the moment.

"Thanks, partner." Clint withdrew his hand.

Nina bit her lip to trap a mew of disappointment.

"Okay, Alex," Clint said with a wink to the boy. "Lead the way. I'm tired and wet, and this leg I busted up in my last rodeo is giving me—"

Nina cleared her throat.

Clint glanced at Nina with a raised brow and straightened his shoulders. "As I was *saying*, my leg is giving me a hard time. I could really use a good night's rest."

Alex rushed from behind the desk and motioned for Clint to follow.

"You can take the lantern," Nina said.

"Thanks."

"C'mon, Clint." Alex turned to lead the man away, then paused and pivoted to face Nina. "Mom? Whose room should I show him to?"

"What do you mean, whose room?" she asked.

"Well," said Alex, putting his hands on his hips to show his impatience with his mother, "is he going to be your roommate or mine?"

"Roommate?" Nina choked on the word and pressed her hand to her chest. As she brushed the nubby fabric, she suddenly recalled that she was wearing her old bathrobe.

Clint chuckled again. "Maybe I should have gone over the terms of our agreement more carefully, Mrs. Jackson. I didn't know I was going to have to share my quarters."

"You don't have to share anything but your advice, Mr. Cooper." She pinched together the lapels of her robe, tossed her head, and pushed past the hulking man to her son.

Next to Alex, she bent down to speak to him eye to eye. "Honey, Mr. Cooper won't be staying in our part of the house. He'll be in the bedroom in the other wing, across the lobby."

"He will?" Even in the dim light, Nina could see her son's eyes grow wide with concern.

As if he saw the same thing, Clint moved forward and leaned down over both of them to address the boy. "It's okay, son, I wouldn't make much of a roomie anyway. My leg isn't fully healed, and it makes me restless some nights."

"I think Mr. Cooper can find his own room." She patted her son on the behind to send him off. "You go back to bed."

"But, he can't…" Alex twisted his head over his shoulder and dug in his heels to keep from leaving.

"I'll be fine, partner," Clint assured him as he stepped back. "You mind your Mama and go on."

Nina let out a long breath.

The light from the lantern in Clint's hand followed him as he moved away, and Nina used the opportunity to slip into the darkness. "Your room is down the hall on the other side of the lobby. The only door on the left."

"Thank you, ma'am."

"I've called a breakfast meeting of the new staff at seven tomorrow morning. I'd like to introduce you to everyone then."

"Fine." Again, he nodded.

"The dining room is just through there." Even though she knew he couldn't see the gesture, she pointed to the arched doorway beside the front desk.

"I'll find it."

"Okay." She retreated a step toward her rooms. "Good night, then."

"'Night." He turned and walked away.

Nina stole one last peek at his retreat, wondering if she'd done the right thing in hiring a man who could rattle her so.

Clint lumbered down the narrow hallway. What had he gotten himself into? A greenhorn boss lady was one thing, but a pretty young thing with a kid? He might have to ask for more money—hazardous duty pay, he believed they called it. Experience told him that this kind of setup was more dangerous than any crazed bronc or charging bull could ever be.

Before he knew it, he speculated, he'd be sucked into their problems and wanting to help out. Need a ranch foreman? *That's me.* Need a handyman? *I'm as handy as they come.* Need a father figure for the boy? *I'm the right age, the right height. Don't worry; whatever you need, ma'am, Clint Cooper is your man.*

Clint shook his head. Wasn't it enough that he'd have to take the tenderfoot gal by the hand and guide her through getting the ranch running? Did he also have to risk getting involved with a family again?

He'd sworn off personal involvement years ago, but something about these two lost lambs made him think that was about to change. Though it wouldn't change his mind about being part of a family again, Clint somehow knew he wouldn't be able to walk away from Jackson's Butte Dude Ranch without losing a part of himself. But what could he do to stop that?

He'd taken the job after a bad throw by a bronc had landed him in the hospital. Even after extensive physical therapy, he didn't have full range of motion in his hip, so he'd come here to try to finish the healing process and to keep his mind off the very real possibility that he would never fully recover. Now he'd found a woman who needed his help just as much, or possibly more, than he needed the distraction of the work. Maybe in his younger days he'd have said a fare-thee-well and hit the road. Maybe. But these days he wasn't the kind of man to back out of a commitment.

Clint lifted the lantern high and checked the doors. He'd found his room and not a moment too soon. He was beat. What he wanted now was sleep—deep, dreamless sleep without visions of a sweet-faced blonde in an old-fashioned nightgown and tattered robe looking for a hero.

Good luck, he told himself, and snorted a sharp chuckle. He whisked his hat off and slapped it against his thigh. Raindrops scattered, landing on the floor and his clothes. One smacked against his neck and skittered downward inside his collar. He shivered.

"Time to hit the hay," he muttered through tight teeth.

He twisted the doorknob and pushed. Nothing happened. The place was old, maybe the door needed a little more persuasion. He placed his shoulder against the slick varnished wood and shoved inward. The door inched open a crack and then stopped. A familiar, overpowering smell greeted him. He'd smelled the trace of horse manure and wet animal in the lobby but assumed he'd tracked something in on his boot heel. Now…

A whinny and the clang of horseshoes on the hard floor confirmed what was inside his room.

"Tell me this isn't happening." Suddenly the door flew open under his weight. Clint stumbled inside and held the lantern aloft.

Two huge, fearful eyes glared at him from beneath a shock of straw-colored hair. A soft, speckled muzzle nudged at the door; large, yellowed teeth flashed. Despite his aching leg, Clint jumped clear of the irate pony, backed into the hallway, and slammed the door between himself and the beast.

"Don't be afraid, Mr. Cooper."

The tiny voice made Clint turn. Alex Jackson stood in the hallway sporting a pair of superhero pajamas.

"That's only Plinkey in your room," Alex explained. "He's a Shetland pony."

"Yeah, I know what it is, kiddo. But how did it get in my room?"

"I put him in there—so he wouldn't be left out in the storm," the child said with obvious pride at this solution.

"That's what stables are for, son," Clint said with extreme patience. "Is this place so broken down it doesn't have one of those?"

"We have one. But I thought Plinkey would be afraid out there all alone." The boy's lower lip quivered.

Something about the expression cut Clint to the quick. The young face reminded him of his own son, opening a wound in Clint that had never properly healed.

He glanced down at the anxious eyes of the boy. Despite his annoyance with his softening heart and the situation, Clint sighed and gave the kid a half smile.

"So you decided to make Plinkey feel better by putting him up in my room?" Clint tried to sound gruff. "Well, isn't that a fine howdy-do for a weary cowpoke?"

"I'm—I'm sorry." The boy's voice was thin, wavering on a broken whisper.

Women who didn't know when to call it quits and kids: those were his only weaknesses. He hated having any weaknesses—especially ones with big blue eyes and even bigger expectations of him. He rolled his eyes heavenward, then decided that no one up there would have any help or sympathy for his predicament.

In fact, he half wondered if the Lord hadn't brought him to this place and to this mom-and-son heart-tugging team. It would have to take some kind of divine intervention to force him to face his pain again like this.

Well, if that was why he was here, it wasn't going to work. No matter how cute Alex Jackson was or how much Nina Jackson needed him, Clint was not going to let down his guard and care about them. And he certainly wasn't going to put his trust in God's plan and risk having his whole world torn away from him again. He just couldn't.

Stiffening, Clint placed a hand on Alex's shoulder and spoke in a firm tone. "A pony doesn't belong in the house, son. He's probably more frightened to be shut in that room than he would be in his familiar stall, even with the storm raging."

"Really?"

"Yep." He nodded and the child mimicked the gesture. "Now, I'm not sure how you got that pony into my room, but you're going to have to help me get him out."

"That's easy." Alex's broad grin rivaled the glow of the lantern. "Plinkey does whatever I want him to."

"Well, that's some comfort," Clint muttered.

Alex started toward the door, then paused and looked back at Clint over his shoulder. "You won't tell my mom, will you, Mr. Cooper?"

Clint grit his teeth. Under normal circumstances, he wouldn't think it right to withhold information from the boy's mother. But the pleading look in the young boy's eyes went straight to his battered heart. He shook his head and heard himself say, "No, I won't breathe a word to your mother, partner."

Together, they worked with the ornery pony until they managed to get it out into the lobby. Just inches from the front door, the animal balked. Lightning scored the sky, followed closely by a boom of thunder.

In one startling moment, the electricity came back on, bringing the outside light to flaring life. At the same time, the headlights from a moving car slashed across the front of the ranch house. Clint welcomed the bright light that flooded the dark room but wondered with some apprehension who would be driving up so late, especially when he was in such a difficult situation.

"Act casual," he growled at the little boy beside him, who was tugging on the pony's mane.

"What's casual?" the boy asked.

Clint gripped the bridle tighter. "Act like pushing a pony through the lobby is something you do all the time—no big deal, like walking a dog."

"But I don't have a dog."

Clint shut his eyes tightly. "Never mind. Just keep Plinkey moving and let me do the talking."

"What an excellent idea, Mr. Cooper. Why don't you start by telling me what you are doing involving my son in your late night shenanigan?"

"Shenanigan?" Clint practically yelped the word. "Me?"

"Yes, you, Mr. Cooper," Nina said, flicking on the overhead light. "And that animal. What are you doing with that animal in the house?"

Clint shifted his weight from his aching leg and groaned under his breath. Shutting his eyes again, he wondered how to answer her question without lying outright or betraying his promise to Alex. When he opened his eyes, he saw Nina Jackson fully for the first time and any explanation he might have offered died on his lips.

Trouble. Blue-eyed, blonde, hands-on-her-hips trouble. That's what he saw. From the glint in her eyes that said she'd stand her own with anyone, to the picture of innocence she made in her long white nightgown covered by a ratty bathrobe, Nina was the kind of woman who could mean nothing but trouble for a man like him.

"Well, Mr. Cooper, I'm waiting for an explanation."

Clint tore his gaze away from her and glanced down at Alex. The boy's pleading eyes all but cried out "I'm counting on you."

He met Nina's gaze again. It was clear she had her expectations of him, too. Obviously, she wanted him to set a good example for her son at the very least, which meant he couldn't stand there and lie his way out of the situation. He did not like this. He did not want this woman or her son to depend on him for anything more than the job he'd been hired to do.

The leather of Plinkey's bridle cut into Clint's palm. The pony strained to twist its head back, its teeth bared. With one jerk of his hand, Clint kept the animal from nipping at him. Why this woman let this young boy have an unruly beast when neither of them seemed to know how to manage it…

Clint turned to face Nina, his grin growing. "Mrs. Jackson, how much do you know about caring for a Shetland?"

"Well, um…" She moved her bare feet on the tile floor and blinked at him. "Not much. That is…nothing."

He nodded. "I thought as much."

"But I do know they don't belong indoors."

"That's true—usually."

"Oh, no." She shook her head, her shining hair swinging against her soft cheek. "You can't convince me that Plinkey needs to be in the house."

"Not that he needs to be," Clint said, patting the horse's broad back. "But since I found him in my room, I can only guess that he's been allowed in the house."

There. That wasn't a lie—not technically, at least. Clint glanced down at Alex and acknowledged the boy's gaping mouth with a wink.

"You don't suppose Plinkey is the reason the front door was open?" Nina asked.

Clint gave her his most earnest expression. "No doubt."

29

"What's going on?" A teenaged girl with light brown hair in two braids bounded into the lobby. "I came back to get my English book, Mrs. Jackson, and I noticed—"

She stopped and stared at the tableau of man, boy, and pony.

"Hey, what's that pony doing in here?" the girl asked.

"Just leaving," Clint said. He tugged at Plinkey's bridle and spoke to Alex. "Go on to bed, son. I'll put Plinkey back in his stall and make sure he can't get out again."

Alex looked up at him, grateful awe shining on his face.

Clint guided the pony outside and started to lead it away, hunching his shoulders against the downpour.

The college girl Nina had hired earlier in the day rushed across the lobby. "I'm really sorry for barging in so late, Mrs. Jackson." She glanced at the clock above the front desk. "Oh my goodness, it's after ten. I wouldn't have come, but I have an assignment to do for tomorrow." She glanced behind her in the direction Clint had gone. "Was that Clint Cooper? What's he doing—"

Nina recalled the young woman's qualifications for the job and her enthusiasm at working with the local hero, Clint Cooper. But it was late and she'd been through quite enough today without having to relate the story of the night's events to anyone. She pointed to the front desk and said quietly, "Your book is right there, Ellen. Come on, Alex, you've had enough adventure for one night."

Alex marched past Ellen, giving a quick good-night wave.

"Wait a minute, pal," Ellen said, bending down. "Tell me, was that man who I thought it was?"

Alex angled his chin up. He grinned. His delighted eyes shone with a happiness Nina hadn't seen in a long time. Then he turned to look out at Clint Cooper tromping through the mud and rain and announced, "Yep. That's my dad."

Chapter TWO

"S o, you see, Alex, when Mr. Cooper called you *son,* it was just an expression." Nina knelt just outside the dining room and looked Alex in the eye.

Members of the staff slowly trickled through the lobby on their way to the breakfast meeting she had called. Quietly, without calling further attention to her problem, she tried to make herself perfectly clear to her son. "Sometimes men call young boys 'son' just like they might call a lady 'honey.' You've heard that before, haven't you?"

Bright morning sunlight poured in the windows across the lobby from them. It reflected off Alex's pale hair as he nodded.

"It doesn't mean anything special, though," Nina said, giving his arms a squeeze. "Mr. Cooper was just trying to be nice."

"He is nice," Alex insisted, his lower lip shoved out in a pout.

"Well, yes, he does seem to be very nice." Clint's heart-stopping smile and kind eyes sprang to her mind. She cocked her head and sighed. "Very nice."

The moment she heard the faraway lilt of her own voice, Nina started. "I mean, he seems quite nice, but that doesn't mean we, that is you, can just claim him for your dad."

"Why not?"

"Why not?"

Nina's surprised squawk drew the attention of a couple of staffers nearby. She cast them a helpless smile and shrugged. When the staff members moved on through the dining room's swinging doors, she took Alex by the hand.

"Alex, we hardly know this man."

"But you said, when we packed up to move here, that we were coming to this ranch to have our own little family. A family has a mommy *and* a daddy."

"Oh, Alex." Nina pulled her son into her arms, resting her cheek against his small chest. She pressed her hand against the back of his head and hugged him close. "Not all families have a mommy and a daddy."

She ached with the sudden realization of how much Alex missed having a father in his life. They'd lost Wayne when Alex was only three years old, and the boy had only vague memories of his father. He had never before shown any indication that he missed Wayne. But Nina had been mistaken, she now understood, to think that just because Alex did not miss his father specifically, that he would not miss having a father—any father.

Her in-laws had tried to keep Wayne alive in the young boy's mind, but Alex simply didn't have enough memories of his father to cling to. In time, the elder Mr. and Mrs. Jackson had given up trying to restore Wayne for Alex and began, instead, to try to recreate their son in their grandchild. That's when Nina knew she had to move on—and when the opportunity to buy the ranch came up.

It had taken all the courage she could muster to ask for the loan to bring her son out here from Kansas City, far from their smothering; but even they had seen the good of a fresh start for the boy—and of owning land. Once they believed that she was building a legacy for their beloved grandson, they had pledged their support.

Nina sighed now as she imagined how they would react if they knew Alex was running around claiming strange men as his father.

She shut her eyes and pressed her cheek to the faint sound of Alex's little heart beating. "Oh, honey, I know you wish you had a daddy, but even so, you just can't pick one out for yourself."

Alex wriggled to loosen her grasp on him. When he had backed away a few inches, he looked down into her eyes and said solemnly, "I didn't pick him out. God did."

"God did?" She blinked and jerked her head back, her hair swinging against her hot cheek.

"Don't you remember?" He scowled in the way only a child can at a parent he thinks has suddenly gone daft. "We prayed for him to send a daddy last night."

Nina raised her gaze to the ceiling and groaned in frustration. How could she handle this without shaking her son's innocent faith? And she had to consider the man in question. How did she make a child understand all the implications of his announcing to Clint that the man was his heaven-sent father? "Alex, I never taught you that prayer is a wish factory. That you can just place an order like the Home Shopping Network."

"There's lotsa places it says so in the Bible," he argued.

"Oh? Like where?" She cocked an eyebrow at him and waited to see how much the tiny Bible scholar might remember of his lessons.

He stared at his toes. "Lotsa places."

This was getting her nowhere. "There's something else you need to consider, young man."

"What?"

"How Mr. Cooper might feel about this, for starters."

"He'll like it," Alex said with a confidence that Nina knew could lead to utter disappointment.

"You don't know that."

Alex scrunched up his face to consider that for the briefest of moments before his expression brightened. "Then I'll just ask him."

"No!" Nina gripped the boy's T-shirt to make sure he didn't suddenly scamper off and proclaim to Clint Cooper that they'd nominated him for father of the year. Or perhaps that should be father of the duration of the ranch job.

Nina fidgeted with the top button of her red gingham western shirt. Alex knew that his own father had left them and gone to heaven; that he hadn't wanted to go but that it was God's plan. How would her son cope when the man he'd hand selected to fill his daddy's shoes left, too, and by the man's own choice? If she allowed Alex to pursue this father fantasy, she was only setting him up for a gigantic heartbreak.

If there were even a chance that she and Clint could...

She brought her forefinger to her mouth and let it rest on her lower lip. No, there was no chance of that. She found the man interesting—there was that classic cowboy mystique about him—and he seemed genuinely nice. He was quite good-looking, and there had been that curious warmth when he'd smiled.... Nina shook her head, irritated with the direction of her thoughts. Love and romance were last on her list of things to do right now. Ahead of those luxuries were other concerns like getting her ranch in order and making loan payments, not to mention the time it took to be a mom to Alex. If she slipped up on the first two, she could very well lose the last one. No man was worth that.

She drew a deep breath, then took Alex firmly by the shoulders. "Alex, no matter how nice a man is, you can't just ask him to be your father. It's way too complicated for Mama to explain right now, with the whole staff gathering for a meeting in a few minutes. But I swear we'll have a long talk about mommies and daddies and falling in love and getting married another time. Okay?"

Alex wrinkled his nose up as though she'd offered him a heaping plate of spinach.

Nina didn't have time to continue this discussion, and yet she couldn't leave the child with expectations about forming a family with a man who'd be gone at the close of the summer season. She brushed a kiss over Alex's cheek, then stood. "Are we clear on this, Alex?"

The boy puffed his cheeks out and let out an impatient sigh that blew his bangs off his forehead.

She crossed her arms and straightened to glower at her uncooperative child. "Are we clear on this, Alex?"

He nodded once, so hard she thought she heard his teeth rattle.

"Good." She gave him a pat on the back. "And not a word of this to Mr. Cooper, okay?"

"Not a word of what to Mr. Cooper?"

Nina swiveled to see Clint strolling toward them. The sight made her chest ache and her head feel light. Washed in early morning sunlight, the man made a powerful presence. Even slightly favoring his right leg, his long stride quickly brought him to them. Nina's gaze swept from his pearl white cowboy hat to his crisp black shirt and faded blue jeans.

He smiled from beneath the shadow of his hat brim and dipped his head in greeting.

Nina bobbed her own head back at him, immediately feeling foolish. She wet her parched lips and managed to smile at Clint. "Good morning. Did you sleep well?"

He shrugged. "Well as could be expected."

She started to ask him if his leg had kept him up, but he dropped his large hand on Alex's head and ruffled the boy's hair.

"So," he said, "what aren't you supposed to tell me? Are you and your mom keeping secrets?"

Nina winced, praying that Alex would not issue an invitation to Clint on the spot to become the head of their family unit.

Alex beamed up at the man. The hero worship in the boy's eyes tugged at Nina's resolve. Ironically, she knew that the male influence would be good for the boy—if they could just keep it in perspective.

"Um, it was only a misunderstanding," she said, stepping closer to Clint to take his attention from Alex. "Nothing to worry about, honestly."

Clint's gaze lifted to her face, growing harder and more serious.

He's on to us. Nina forced a bright smile to cover her apprehension that Clint suspected they'd been having a personal discussion about him. To her relief, Ellen walked onto the scene just then.

"Oh, Ellen, I'm glad you're here." She snagged the girl by the arm. "Would you take Alex in and help him get some breakfast? Mr. Cooper and I need a moment alone."

"I'll bet you do," Ellen said with a mischievous smile. She reached out and took Alex by the hand to lead him into the dining room. "C'mon, tiger, let's get you some grub. I have a feeling you're going to be a very popular kid around the breakfast table this morning."

"What was that all about?" Clint asked as they watched the pair disappear through the swinging doors into the large dining room.

"I think Ellen is just trying to make Alex feel good about his new home," Nina replied, hoping that was all there was to the girl's cryptic remark.

"No, I don't mean that." Clint jerked his head toward the room where Alex and Ellen had gone. "I mean, what's all that about not telling Mr. Cooper? You two weren't planning a surprise party for my birthday, were you? Because if you were, I can tell you now that I like my cake chocolate, my ice cream vanilla, and my presents expensive."

Nina blinked at him. "We weren't… I wasn't even aware that it was your birthday. But maybe I could have the cook bake a cake and…"

A broad, "gotcha" grin broke over Clint's face.

"Oh." Nina bounced the toe of her red canvas shoe against the floor. Despite the urge to jab the man in the ribs for stringing her along, she had to laugh.

He laughed, too. Then they both fell into an awkward silence.

"Um, I guess I—sort of—owe you an apology for my behavior last night," Nina finally said.

"No, you—sort of—don't."

Hearing her own qualification made Nina feel silly.

"You acted like any normal mama bobcat defending her young. I guess I should just count myself lucky that you weren't wielding anything more lethal than a book, huh?" He smiled at her and adjusted his hat.

She bowed her head for a moment. "I just hope we'll be able to work well together, even if we did get off to a bad start."

His lean cheek twitched with restrained tension. His eyes searched her face.

She shifted under the weight of his open scrutiny, waiting for his verdict.

He skimmed his hand along the brim of his hat and sighed. His expression softened. "I don't see why we can't keep from killing one another, if that's what you're asking."

"Good." She gave a quick nod. "I've got everything riding on making this ranch work, Mr. Cooper. I don't think I can do that without your help."

"Everything?" He hooked his thumbs in his belt loops and scowled. "You're saying you've staked everything you have on a run-down ranch and a beat-up cowboy?"

Nina cast her gaze downward. She didn't believe that either he or the ranch were in such bad shape as he claimed, but that wasn't the issue here. The issue was letting him know how important it was that she make the ranch work. To do that, she had to be perfectly honest with him.

"I borrowed a lot of money to buy this ranch, Mr. Cooper. I have a good amount that I've saved to go toward the fix-up process, but I have to at least break even by the end of tourist season, or else."

His brow crimped over his clear brown eyes. "Or else? You sound like you borrowed money from the types who break your legs if you don't pay up."

"Worse."

"Worse?"

"I borrowed from my in-laws."

"You look smarter than that," he teased.

"What else could I do?" She gestured with open hands. "No bank would make that kind of loan to a single mom taking on a new business in this economy."

"And that didn't send up a red flag that maybe this wasn't the greatest idea?"

"It is a great idea," she insisted. "And it will work. I'll have a great first season and make my first loan payment with money to spare." She raised her eyebrows as if to challenge him to disagree with her optimistic attitude. When he kept his peace, she continued. "Luckily, Mr. Cooper, you don't have to share my vision to help me realize it."

All of Clint's misgivings from the night before came flooding back. He sighed. Women who didn't know when to give up when it was the only sensible thing to do—they got to him every time. Clint gazed at Nina's proud expression.

He stepped just a bit closer than necessary to her and inhaled the fresh scent of the shampoo in her silken hair. Little feminine touches like that were what he'd missed most in the years since his wife died. He'd been too young to appreciate them then. But now, after five years of purposefully blocking out the sweet incidentals in the few women he had dated, Clint couldn't seem to keep himself from trying to absorb as much as he could of Nina's scent, her delicate gestures, the softness of her.

"So, what's it to be, Mr. Cooper? Are you going to help me make Jackson's Butte Western Dude Ranch a success?"

"Clint."

She paused, lifted her unassuming gaze to his, then lowered her thick lashes over her luminous eyes.

"Please," he urged in a whisper, "call me Clint."

She wet her lips and smiled faintly. "Okay, Clint."

Her voice rasped against his frazzled nerves. The hair on the back of his neck rose in response to her voice wrapping so delicately around his name.

She dipped her head slightly. "And you can call me Nina."

"I always have," he reminded her in a husky voice.

"Yes, well." She cleared her throat. "You still haven't answered my question. Are you ready to help me make this the best dude ranch in southern Colorado?"

"I'll do my best, ma'am," he murmured, wondering how he could temper her enthusiasm with a dose of reality without wounding her admirable spirit. Finally, he settled for smiling at her as he nodded. "I think with your attitude and my know-how, we can whip this place into shape."

"Good." She put her hand on his arm. "I'm counting on you."

I'm in this up to my hindquarters now. He looked into Nina's sparkling blue eyes.

Her fingers flexed gently into the taut muscle of his forearm.

A million burning embers shot through his system. Who was he kidding? He was in this up to his freshly steamed and blocked custom-made cowboy hat.

"Now, shall we go in and meet the rest of the staff?" she asked with a smile so sweet it made his teeth ache.

"Lead me on," he said, clearly aware of the double meaning.

She moved ahead of him and headed toward the dining room.

Maybe, he told himself, he could survive this unscathed. Maybe he'd find he didn't give a hoot what happened to this rattletrap ranch, this pretty lady, or her terrific kid. Maybe he could just do his job and get out—no mess; no entanglements of any kind.

His gaze drifted over the swing of Nina's hair, the optimistic spring in her step.

Yeah, and maybe later he'd put on a pink tutu and dance like the Sugarplum Fairy. There was about as much chance of that happening as there was that he'd escape from his encounter with Nina Jackson with his time-toughened defenses intact.

Nina pushed open one of the dining room's swinging doors, then paused to ask, "Will you want to say a few words to the staff? I know they're all very excited about your being here."

Rich aromas of food and coffee wafted over him, making his mouth water and his stomach grumble. Silverware clattered against plates. Voices and laughter rose in quiet chaos as the staff members enjoyed their meal.

"I'm not much for speech making, especially on an empty stomach. Maybe after breakfast."

"Fair enough." She nodded and shouldered the door fully open.

They stepped inside the bustling dining room side by side. The door fell shut behind them with a whoosh, drawing some attention. In what seemed like a split second, everything went silent and still. All eyes were on them.

Clint surveyed the faces gaping at them. He counted sixteen young men and women, all appearing to be in their late teens or early twenties.

"Looks like your legend has preceded you, Mr.—um, Clint."

Young men stared at him, some with open admiration, some with the gleam of challenge in their eyes. The girls' eyes also shone at him with regard, a couple with a blatant interest that he'd learned to ignore. During his years on the rodeo circuit, he'd discovered that some women seemed to think cowboys lived more exciting lives than other men. He wasn't sure where they got that misconception.

He cleared his throat uneasily. "Aw, they're no more interested in me than they are in you. After all, you are the new boss lady."

"I have eyes, you know."

He glanced down at her. His chest constricted for a moment. "Yeah, I noticed your eyes."

She tossed her head and her hair rippled around her face. "I can plainly see the kids are in awe of you—Clint Cooper, the cowboy of mythical proportions."

He let a sly grin slide along his lips. "Why, thank you, ma'am. And I thought you were just interested in my abilities as a ranch hand."

Nina's eyes grew dark as they opened wide in shock, followed by a deep pink flush that spread over her cheeks. When she answered him, her words rushed out in a hiss. "I meant your reputation, you—big galoot."

"Hey, now, watch your language, young lady," he teased, his eyebrows arched high in mock warning.

"And you watch my temper," she suggested with just the hint of a smile on her lips and in her eyes.

There were other things about her that he'd rather watch, but he decided against telling her that. Instead he said, "Oh, I think I'm safe here. There isn't an English book within a mile of this dining room."

She rolled her eyes at the lame jest, shook her head, then started forward.

Clint followed, disregarding the few lingering stares of the staff.

Without warning, Nina stopped. Clint tried to stop himself but couldn't keep from running into her.

She stiffened. "Listen, Clint. It's clear the staff has a certain perception of you, and that's good. But I don't want their admiration for you to upstage my role as ranch owner."

"Makes sense." He stepped back slightly to keep from touching her but remained close enough to share the hushed discussion.

She twisted her head to speak over her shoulder to him. "I want you and everyone on the staff to understand that your input is important, but the final word is mine."

He grinned down on her. "Far be it from me to try to keep a woman from having the final word, ma'am."

She pressed her lips together as her eyes narrowed and shifted.

To her credit, she didn't launch into an argument. Nope, she wouldn't be the type to let him justify his sexist remark by her own actions. He liked this woman, and he was going to do whatever he could to help her make her business boom. He deferred to her with a nod and said, "I'll make sure everyone knows you're the boss, Nina. Don't worry."

"Thank you."

As they moved through the dining room, waves of quiet conversation stopped and then started in their wake.

Clint tried several times to make eye contact, but every time he did, the person gawked at him or quickly looked away.

"Something's up. Something more than just curiosity about a rodeo champion or the new boss," he told Nina as they reached the serving line.

She pushed a plastic tray into his midsection. "Nonsense. They're a little starstruck, that's all."

Clint placed the tray on the long stainless steel bars in front of the cafeteria-style steam tables. He slid it along, selecting some flatware rolled in a scratchy white napkin and depositing it on the tray. "It's more than that, but I just can't put my finger on it."

"Then put your finger on this." She accepted a plate the server was handing under the plastic sneeze guard. The heavy white ceramic dish clunked onto the plastic tray.

Clint glanced down at the offering. "What's this?"

"Breakfast." Nina reached out and plunked two small juice bottles onto their respective trays.

"Whose breakfast?" Clint asked, examining the exotic fruit listed on the bottle's label.

Nina gave the server an embarrassed, tight smile, then moved on, whispering harshly, "Your breakfast."

"I don't think so. Where's my fried eggs? Where's my bacon? Where's my steaming hot coffee with cream?"

"We don't have bacon and eggs, but if you want coffee, there's decaf and powdered creamer on that side table over there." She nodded to the right, then lifted her tray and began to walk toward one of the many tables scattered around the room.

Clint scoffed at the table with its green brimmed coffeepot and baskets of creamer packets and sugar substitutes. In a few short steps, he met up with Nina as she settled into a chair.

Still holding his tray, he scowled down at her. "This is just a temporary thing, right? I can see not having a full menu with just the staff here, but once you're open to guests you'll have bacon and eggs and real coffee and cream, right?"

She stabbed her fork into a piece of the Belgian waffle on her plate and lifted it to her lips. "I don't plan on it, no." She popped the bite into her mouth.

Clint set his tray down on the table with a thunk. He should have seen this coming, but he'd been too distracted by the personal side of this arrangement to put much thought into the business end. Now he saw that more than just helping Nina get her ranch running, he would have to help her with a few more basic aspects—like giving the place a western flavor.

Sighing, he pulled back the chair opposite her and swung his leg over to sit down. "What did you plan on calling this place again, Nina?"

"Jackson's Butte Western Dude Ranch," she said slowly. Her voice sounded more than a little annoyed.

"Western?" He rested his forearms against the edge of the table and leaned in. "Did you or did you not just say 'Western'?"

"You know I did."

"And what kind of waffles have we here?" He tipped up the plate to display the fluffy pastry centered there.

"Belgian." She ground out the word through a tight grimace.

"And in what part of the West do we find Belgium?" He let the plate fall back to the table none too gently.

44

"Look, Clint, I get your point, but there are other things I had to take into account when setting the menus here." She poked at her own waffle. "These are my chef's specialty."

"Well, there's your problem right there, lady." He set an elbow on the table and rested his chin in his hand, narrowing one eye on her. "Ranches don't have chefs, they have cooks— preferably grizzled old characters with voices like gravel against pig iron."

Nina winced in distaste. "My chef happens to be very good. He specializes in healthy cooking that I think my guests will appreciate."

"If your guests wanted healthy, they'd go to a spa, not a dude ranch," he said quietly. "Your guests will come here expecting cowboy cooking—bacon and eggs with real coffee. That's authentic fare."

"Well," she said, shoving the waffle around on her plate, "perhaps I could get the chef to prepare a turkey bacon and egg substitute quiche."

He shut his eyes. "I'm going to pretend I didn't hear that."

"Hey, at least I'm offering a compromise. What more do you want from me?"

"Real coffee, real bacon, and real eggs would be good—for a start."

"Caffeine, fat, and cholesterol?" She tossed her napkin onto the table, but Clint did not make the mistake of seeing that as a white flag. She straightened her slender shoulders and her pretty eyes flashed at him. "You want me to serve my guests heart attacks on a platter? Those foods are killers, Clint."

"Look, lady," he said through gritted teeth. "You hired me to help add a western flavor to your dude ranch. And I'm telling you that the flavor of the West is bacon grease."

She glowered at him.

He shrugged and chuckled without humor. "If you're not

even going to listen to my suggestions…"

He left the threat unfinished.

"I hired you to help me with the ranch details, not the kitchen," she replied. "If you can't handle that, then…"

She, too, didn't need to complete the thought.

Clint lifted his head and moved as close to her as the table would permit. The chair screeched against the polished hardwood floor. He leaned in until his face was only inches from hers. "Don't try to bluff with me, lady. I already know your hand. You need me—bad. Without me, you can't make a go of this ranch, and we both know that's not an option for you."

Her sparkling eyes bore into his steady gaze.

"Now, my suggestion to you is to change your menu," he said. "Are you going to take my expert advice or not?"

Nina pushed her chair back and stood to look down on him. The tilt of her chin told him that this was not an unconditional surrender.

"Aw, c'mon, Nina, it's not that bad. After all, nobody's going to die over one little breakfast."

She tossed her blonde hair and spun on her heel, muttering just loud enough for him to hear as she left, "If I were you, Clint Cooper, I wouldn't be too sure of that."

Chapter THREE

Clint strode out from the main building into the warm afternoon sun and stopped. He inhaled the fresh spring air, then twisted his head to peer behind himself.

"What's wrong?" Nina asked over the banging of the front door as she joined him outside.

Clint pushed his hat to the back of his head and chuckled. "I believe that's the first time since I started work here yesterday morning that I've made a sudden stop and didn't have a little face bumping into the back of my leg."

Nina's warm expression cooled by several degrees. She jerked her chin up and crossed her arms over her light gray T-shirt bearing the ranch logo. "If you don't want Alex tagging along, just say so. After all, it's so unlike you to keep your opinion about anything to yourself."

Clint turned his face heavenward for a moment, sighed, then dropped his gaze to Nina. "If I've seemed to nitpick, Nina, it's been for your own good."

"Why, thank you so much for looking out for me by demanding I eat unhealthy food and keeping my blood pressure high by arguing with me over every idea I have for the ranch." The bright sun glinted off her hair and highlighted the faint pink of the sunburn on her nose and cheeks. She shifted her hips and tapped the toe of her tennis shoe on the grassy ground.

Clint couldn't help noticing how nice she looked in her new blue jeans. Clenching his jaw, he coughed to clear the dryness in his throat. "I haven't argued over every point, Nina. You have a lot of good ideas."

She raised one eyebrow at him.

"Unfortunately, very few of them are feasible for your first year. If you really want to make this place work, you'll have to spend your limited funds on things like an emergency generator, renovations, and livestock. You can't waste money on frills like color brochures and expanding the dining room."

"Yes, yes, I've heard your case against the expansion," she said, her battered pride showing. "So, thank you for doing your job. I'll give your advice all the consideration it deserves. That's all you need to know."

So far, she hadn't given even the slightest indication that she'd follow his suggestions or that she even gave them more than a passing thought. That did not bode well for the ranch. Not that it mattered one bit to him if she fell on her pretty little nose, no, sirree. He shook his head. "Fine, lady, it's your grave."

"What's that supposed to mean?" She glared at him, tucking a stray lock of blonde hair behind one ear.

He shrugged. "You're right. You can totally disregard every recommendation I make. And I can't do a thing about it. You hired me as a foreman, not a baby-sitter."

"So, now we're back to Alex." She drew up her shoulders and laced her arms over her chest. "I suppose you want me to tell him to leave you alone?"

"I meant I wasn't hired to baby-sit you, lady." He looked up at her and rested his hands on his hips. "Alex is fine. I don't mind having him along. When I mentioned him earlier, I was just kidding about how it seemed every time I turn around, the half-pint is right there."

Nina's rigid stance relaxed a bit. She glanced down, then raised her gaze to his, a glimmer of reconciliation in her eyes. "I'm sorry I jumped to the wrong conclusion. The deeper I get into the ranch business, the more stress I feel. It's beginning to take its toll."

"That's understandable," he said softly. "And that's precisely why going out to inspect the riding paths will be good for you today."

She smiled and stretched. "Yes, I can't wait to get in the saddle and get a tour of my place on horseback. Getting out from behind my desk will feel great."

"Great," Clint echoed, trying not to notice how the warm sunlight bathed her creamy complexion.

"And about Alex. I really will try to keep him out of your hair more." She moved close enough to Clint to rest her hand on his forearm, bared by his rolled-up sleeve.

"Really, don't worry about it."

"No, he's overdoing it a bit. I don't want him to be—" She stopped herself, wrinkling her nose as though unsure of what to say.

"He's not a pest," Clint assured her. "He's a terrific kid."

"Yes, he is." Her features softened with motherly love. "And he thinks the world of you. You've become quite a role model for him. He hasn't had many of those."

So, she hadn't brought many other men into the boy's life since she'd been widowed. That knowledge induced all sorts of masculine reactions—pride, satisfaction, possessiveness. None of them were very progressive and had no place in his business relationship with Nina, but he couldn't help feeling them anyway.

He scuffed his boot on a patch of dirt. "Don't know that I'm comfortable being a role model."

"Maybe role model isn't the right word."

"Oh?"

The twinkle in her blue eyes told him she was no longer annoyed with him and was ready to have a little fun. "Actually, if I were to characterize the way Alex thinks of you, it would be…"

"Ornery old fool?" he offered, playing along.

"Hmm." She stroked her chin. "That may be an accurate label," she teased, "but for some reason, Alex sees you differently."

"Yeah, well, he does look up to me—literally."

"Good point." She tapped her fingertip to her lips, drawing Clint's attention. "However, if I had to pin a name on how Alex thinks of you, I'd have to say it's more akin to a superhero."

"A superhero? Like Superman?" Clint snorted in feigned disgust. "You mean he sees me as some fellow who would run around in a cape and tights? I don't think so."

"You mean you'd rather be a superhero who runs around without tights?" She shook her head, laughing. "Uh-uh. I'm afraid I'm not running that kind of ranch."

Clint couldn't help chuckling.

"But maybe that is the solution to one of our ranch problems."

"What?" he asked in shock.

"Having a superhero as a mascot." She wriggled her eyebrows at him. "We already have a resident western legend; it would only take a little fabric and imagination to elevate your status."

"What would you call me?" He folded his arms over his chest and cocked his head at her, letting her have her fun. "Raggedy Old Cowpoke Man?"

She shook her head, the sunlight skimming bright over her hair. "That lacks oomph."

"Oomph?" He winced. "Sounds like what I say when I get thrown by a bronc."

"You know what I mean." She cast him a quick, teasing glance. "Now, use your imagination."

"Actually, I'm trying not to," he muttered, inhaling the scent of her sun-warmed skin.

"I can make a costume." She made a quick study of him. "I see you in something red—with an animal on the front of your shirt."

"An animal?"

"Yes, something western." She bit her lip. "I know, a steer. We could put a great big steer's head on your shirt."

"A steer?" He swallowed hard and dragged his splayed fingers through the curls along the back brim of his hat. "I don't think so, Nina."

"Oh, it would be great. We'd put up a big sign." She nudged him to show she was still swept up in the jest. She spread her hands wide as though reading a billboard. "Welcome to Jackson's Butte Dude Ranch—home of Steerman."

Instinctively, Clint's legs tightened, his knees practically locking together. "Would you stop saying that?"

"Why?" She flattened her hands to his chest and tipped her head back, her full lips curved into a mischievous smile. "Afraid you can't live up to the name?"

"Hardly." He barked a laugh. "What I'm afraid of, in point of fact, is that I've taken a job with a woman who fancies herself a rancher and doesn't even know what a steer is."

"It's one of those…" She pulled her hands from his chest and pantomimed horns at the sides of her head.

He took her by the upper arms, shaking his head.

"It's not one of these?" She crooked her fingers and wriggled them.

Clint smiled at her antics, then shook his head at her.

51

"Nina, a steer is a bull that has been—um—emasculated."

Her lips formed a soundless oh.

"I may be busted up, my career may be on hold, and I may be playing nursemaid to a tenderfoot boss lady and her little boy," he told her quietly, "but that doesn't make me a steer. Not by a long shot."

She blinked her enormous eyes at him.

He was going to kiss her. He told her so with his nearness, with his steady, shallow breathing, and with the longing look in his deep brown eyes. He was going to pull her into those big strong arms, crush her to him, and kiss her.

And she was going to let him.

Let him? If he didn't hurry she might just beat him to the pucker, she realized. Knowing it was wrong, she wet her lips in anticipation and wound her fingers into the crisp cotton of his shirt. She swayed closer to him and held her breath, wondering why he didn't make his move.

Then he did.

He gripped her arms and set her firmly away from him. "If we're going to hit the riding trails today, we'd better get going."

"Riding trails?" she murmured, still dazed.

"Isn't that the plan for the day?" He slipped his hat from his head and fiddled with the hatband for a moment. Then he cleared his throat and replaced the hat lightly over his sweat-dampened hair. "You do still want to go on a trail ride, don't you?"

Embarrassed at her uncharacteristically forward behavior— she had practically asked for a kiss from her ranch foreman, for goodness' sake—Nina looked everywhere but at the man when she answered him. "Sure. I still want to go. If it's not any trouble for you."

"It's no trouble."

The note of sadness in his tone compelled her to look at

him. Their gazes held for a few seconds more than comfortable, then she broke eye contact for an instant. When her gaze flitted back, his brown eyes remained intensely focused on her.

So, he had wanted to kiss her. Then why had he stopped himself? Did he feel the need to protect her from her own lapse in common sense? Or perhaps he was simply showing the kind of moral reserve she should have used herself. Nina wondered if she would ever know.

Finally, Clint glanced away. He narrowed his eyes at the horizon, then at the barn. "You never did tell me where my half-pint shadow is this morning."

Nina exhaled, unaware of how long she had held her breath. "Um, Alex is with Plinkey. He was going to get him ready to be saddled."

"Saddled? What for?"

Nina leaned her shoulders back and crossed her arms. "You said Alex could go on the trail ride with us, Clint."

"Yeah, I remember inviting the kid, but I don't recall including that pony."

Nina grinned. "Plinkey is Alex's horse, Clint. They're a package deal."

Clint groaned, his face tilted skyward. "This is going to be a very long ride."

"I'm surprised you can ride at all, after your encounter with Plinkey yesterday afternoon," she teased.

Rubbing one hand over his backside, Clint smiled. "Luckily, the beast didn't do more than nip the skin through my jeans."

"Plinkey seems to have an instinct to protect my son. You never should have picked Alex up with that watch-horse on duty." She poked her hands into her pockets and tried not to take too much pleasure in recalling the incident.

"Yeah, well, that pony better watch out—I'm thinking

about wearing a cast-iron skillet back there from now on."

"Oh, that should be attractive." Laughter broke through her taut smile.

"It beats the getup you were trying to put me in, lady." He joined her laughter.

"I hate to intrude," Ellen called as she approached them, "but I need you to sign this invoice, Mrs. Jackson."

"I guess I'll go see if I can get that pony saddled without having to file for workmen's compensation." Clint tipped his hat to the ladies.

"Watch your back," Nina warned.

"Don't worry, ma'am. That expression 'once bitten, twice shy' is my motto."

Nina forced her gaze up to meet his. He meant something more than just the way he intended to handle the Shetland pony. If she hadn't already known that, one look in his chillingly serious eyes would have confirmed it. She pressed her lips tightly together and gave him a curt nod.

"I'll join you in the barn in a few minutes." If she had said it in more than a whisper, it would have sounded fine. Businesslike. Instead it sounded lost and sad. Nina sighed.

Clint touched two fingers to the brim of his hat, then turned and headed for the barn.

Ellen thrust a clipboard toward Nina, and she accepted it without taking her eyes off Clint. She chuckled again, thinking of his threat to wear a skillet in his jeans. It would be more worthwhile if she could get him to put a lid on his constant faultfinding with her plans for the ranch.

The man exhausted her. He made the mountains of work she faced seem twice as large and impossible to overcome. Still, she had to admit that nearly every suggestion the man made was valid and would be better for the ranch in the long run.

"The first delivery of bacon and eggs arrived, Mrs. Jackson.

I need you to sign the invoice."

Nina flipped through the multicolored papers on the clipboard, her eyes glossing over the columns of quantities and prices. Finally, she sighed and shook her head. How could she concentrate on numbers when her mind was on Clint Cooper? "This is ridiculous."

"It's the coffee," Ellen said with authority. "More than one of the staffers has said the caffeine makes them jittery."

Nina smiled with just a trace of smugness. "Tomorrow, let's make two pots, then—regular and decaf, okay?"

"Sure."

"Now, about these invoices." Nina pulled out the ballpoint pen that was attached to the clipboard. "Does everything seem to be in order?"

"Everything checks out. But I don't know when I've ever seen so much pork fat." Ellen wrinkled her nose.

"Yes, and we can all send our medical bills to Clint. If the cholesterol doesn't give him a heart attack, maybe that will." Nina scrawled her name across the bottom of the first page.

Ellen gaped at her with wide eyes. "You don't really want Mr. Cooper to have a heart attack, do you?"

"No," she admitted with a chuckle. "But I wouldn't mind if he suffered a bout of laryngitis."

Ellen grinned and hunched her shoulders up. "Not like you two need to talk to communicate, huh?"

Nina handed the clipboard back to the girl. "I don't know what you mean, Ellen."

"Nothing, just a joke." She tilted her head questioningly. "It doesn't seem like you two are trying awfully hard to…work things out."

"*Work* being the key word." Nina sighed. "But I have to tell you, that man isn't exactly the king of compromise."

"Everything will be all right, Mrs. Jackson, I'm sure. Too

much is at stake for you not to sort things through."

Finally, someone who understood and appreciated her situation. "I truly do believe that all things work for the good of those who love the Lord, Ellen. If I didn't, I don't think I could get out of bed some days. And your support really means a lot, too."

"Oh, the whole staff is rooting for you—for both you and Mr. Cooper."

Both of them. The wording nagged at Nina even as she rode with Clint and Alex along the overgrown trails in the sloping range beyond the dude ranch proper. Of course the staff would root for her to make the ranch a success—their jobs depended upon it. And they knew Clint was part of making that happen; that's all there was to it. She didn't believe a word of the justification but knew she was foolish to fret over it.

"You're awfully quiet," Clint said, bringing his horse, Ranger, alongside hers.

She patted the neck of the aging palomino beneath her and shifted her weight, her saddle creaking. The horse shook its pale mane and snorted. "I'm just trying to sort a few things out," she said with a shrug.

"You're worried about the state of the trails, aren't you?" He glanced behind them at Alex and Plinkey plodding happily along, then turned back to her. "I know the paths look bad, Nina, but they really aren't."

"Really?" Coming from him, that positive statement meant something. "How long would it take for us to get them in shape?"

Clint stroked his jaw. "That depends on how many staffers we commit to the task. I figure that half a dozen kids can clear out the worst of the best paths in a few days."

"The worst of the best?" She arched one brow. "And what about the other trails?"

"We'll get to them as we can." He narrowed his eyes in the shadow of his hat brim and studied the winding trail ahead.

"But they'll all be open before the season begins, right?"

"Nina, be reasonable." He shook his head.

Nina leaned back in the saddle and pulled hard on the reins to bring her horse to a halt.

Clint accomplished the same feat with Ranger with such grace it seemed almost telepathic.

Behind them, Alex roared out, "Whoa. Whoa, Plinkey."

The boy's small legs, which poked almost straight out from the back of the plump pony, jounced against the horse's ribcage.

Clint bent his head to disguise his humor at the picture. "Use the reins the way I taught you, Alex," he called out in a calm voice. "And try to keep your legs still so Plinkey won't get a mixed message."

Alex finally got the pony to stop. He beamed proudly at Nina, then fixed a curious scowl on Clint. "What's a mixed message?"

Nina thought back to the kiss that didn't materialize and smiled to herself. If her son wanted to know about a mixed message, he had come to the master.

"A mixed message is like if you ask me for some candy and I say yes, then put the candy out of your reach," Clint responded.

"You'd never do that," Alex said with a giggle.

Don't bet he wouldn't, Nina thought.

"Well, if I did, I'd be sending you a mixed message, and you'd have a hard time knowing what to do about it."

He wouldn't be the only one, she mused, studying Clint's lips.

Alex raised his small hand to shade his eyes as he squinted in the glaring sunlight.

"What's the matter, partner?" Clint asked, cocking his head.

57

"Do you mean to tell me your mom spent a fortune buying a dude ranch and hiring a professional cowboy and didn't pop for a cowboy hat for you?"

Alex held his hands out and shrugged.

"Talk about your mixed messages." Clint glanced at her with a teasing lift to his brows.

Nina guiltily adjusted her sunglasses on her nose. "I told Alex to wear a baseball cap, but he didn't listen."

"Good for him." Clint shook his head at her, his expression dour but his eyes glinting. "No self-respecting cowpoke would be caught wearing a ball cap on a trail ride."

"Well, there's nothing we can do about it now," she said, fighting a stab of shame at her oversight.

"Of course there is." Clint turned his horse around with ease and guided him next to Alex and Plinkey.

The Shetland lunged for Clint's leg as he brushed past but didn't get a bite. When the horses were aligned, Plinkey got a faceful of Ranger's tail for his sassiness. Clint and Alex shared a laugh as they watched the pony shake his head.

The sight of the two males getting along so well made Nina's heart swell. Alex had seemed happier these past two days than he had in a long, long time. And that was the mixed message she had to deal with. She had to make sure Alex understood that no matter how strong the bond between them grew, Clint was a mentor, a role model, even a friend—but he was not and never would be his father.

"Here you go, son." Clint lifted his own hat and plunked it down on Alex's white blond head.

The hat fell over the boy's eyes and stopped just above his tiny bump of a nose.

"A perfect fit," Clint announced.

A peal of giggles came from under the hat, making it shake and wobble.

Clint whooped out a laugh, too.

A tight, dry chuckle that sounded more like a cough caught in Nina's chest. Much as she wanted to rush forward and involve herself, to warn Alex not to read too much into the gesture, she held back. The way to handle this was during her private moments with Alex, when she could emphasize, in a firm but positive way, the temporary nature of Clint's presence in their lives. For now…

For now she just wanted to let Alex have his fun.

Alex pushed the hat back to reveal his face and grinned at Clint.

"Do you think you can manage that big old hat, partner?"

Alex gave a quick nod. The hat fell forward and covered his eyes again. Once more, the boy squealed with laughter.

Clint leaned over and placed the hat just so on the boy's head and it stayed as if by magic. He gave Alex a wink, then turned Ranger and joined Nina again.

"Thanks," she said quietly.

"Don't mention it."

He sounded as if he meant that literally, so she let it go. "Okay, now where were we?"

"About to finish our trail ride?" he asked hopefully.

"As I recall, we were about to finish a discussion on opening the riding paths." She lowered her chin and nailed him with a glare.

"Nina, we can't have all the trails open for the beginning of the season. If we're lucky, we'll have most of them open by the end of it." He folded his hands over the horn of his saddle. "There are a few that can't be opened this year at all, though."

"And those would be?" She raised one eyebrow at him.

"The mountain trails."

"The mountain trails!"

He twisted around in his saddle to ask Alex, "Hey, sport, do you hear an echo around here?"

Holding the huge hat in place with one hand, Alex shook his head.

"Quit clowning, and listen to me," she snapped. "I have to have the mountain trails open—if not all of them, at least one or two."

"Why?"

"Why?"

He craned his neck to shout over his shoulder again, "Partner, are you sure you don't hear an echo?"

"No, sir. No echo," was the report from Alex.

Nina gritted her teeth and ignored his wisecracking. "I need the mountain trails because guests will want to use them. One of the charms of a ranch in this part of the country is the mix of western flavor and mountain scenery."

"I'm not saying they can't enjoy the scenery," Clint answered. "Just that they can't take the trails. If they feel like hiking and climbing, they can ride out to that puny thing you call Jackson's Butte."

"As I'm sure they will, but I need those trails open for more than just hiking."

"Like what?"

"Like access to the mountain cabins."

"The what?"

"The mountain cabins. The previous owners told me I could get to them by truck if I needed to, but there are trails leading to all five of them."

Clint shook his head, the sun highlighting the golden threads in his hair. "I doubt if it would be worth the trouble to even bother with them this first season, Nina."

"But the old brochures called those cabins 'quaint and rustic, ideal for individual family camping adventures.'" She gripped the reins in her hand and jiggled her feet in the stirrups.

Her horse took one faltering step forward.

"Whoa," Clint said softly to the palomino. It immediately obeyed. Then he focused his calming gaze on her. "Those brochures also called a chipped concrete tipi and ratty stuffed buffalo an authentic Native American village display. I'd be afraid to hazard a guess at what they'd consider quaint and rustic."

Nina's pulse pounded with anxiety. How could she make Clint understand how desperately she needed to open the mountain cabins, how much she needed the revenue they could provide? "B-but, I have to—"

A shrill beeping interrupted Nina's plea.

"What's that?" Clint scowled.

"I have a pager and a cellular phone so no matter where I am on the ranch, I can always maintain touch with the staff," Nina said as she pressed a button on the pager. "I know it's not the 'western' way to do things, but I thought it made sense."

"I agree."

"You do?" Nina paused in the middle of dialing the ranch number on the phone.

"Is it so shocking that I might agree with you from time to time?"

She simply shook her head and continued with her call. The phone conversation only took a few moments.

"What? What is it, Nina?" Clint leaned toward her. "You look like you've seen a ghost."

She managed to wrest her gaze from the receiver cradled in her palm. It took her a few seconds to get Clint's face fully in focus, so many thoughts were racing in her mind.

"What is it, Nina?"

She licked her parched lips and inhaled the scent of horses, dirt, and foliage. "The decision about the mountain cabins will have to wait."

"Is there an emergency back at the ranch?"

"I don't know," she answered numbly.

"Would you just tell me what's the matter, then?"

"It may be nothing. Or it may be the end of everything I hoped to build here."

"Talk sense," he said softly.

She raised her gaze to his concerned eyes and let her bottom lip slide from under her teeth. "The message is that I have a certified letter back at the ranch house. It's from my in-laws."

"That isn't necessarily bad news, you know." He patted her leg and smiled.

"No, not necessarily," she agreed in a small, faraway voice. She stole a peek at Alex over her shoulder. "But in the eight years I've known them, I've never—not once—known them to be the bearers of good news—especially where I was concerned."

Chapter FOUR

Well?" Clint stood in the narrow doorway of Nina's cramped office, his shoulders nearly touching the frame on either side.

He watched as she refolded the papers in her hand, crimping them between her pinched thumb and forefinger to put a sharp edge on the crease. She placed the corner of the letter to her lips and tapped.

Clint knew he had no business in here. No business questioning her about the contents of her certified letter. Why would he want to know anyway? It sure didn't concern him. He was just a hired hand around the place. Whatever went on between Nina and her in-laws held no interest for him.

He dipped his chin to study the delicate blonde boss lady from beneath the brim of his hat. Whatever was in that letter sure had her flustered.

Not that he cared one whit about the gal's emotional state or her volatile relationship with her in-laws. It wasn't his lookout. He had no intention of getting involved.

"Nina?" he asked, the heel of his boot scuffing the threshold.

"Hmm?" She blinked at him. *At* him, as if she didn't really see him at all.

Even though they weren't focused on him, those eyes reached straight into his chest and touched his heart. Nina awakened in him things he had too long forgotten. And he hated it. Hated it—and longed with every fiber in his being to seek out her gaze and the emotions it raised as often as possible.

He drew a deep breath of dry, musty air and cleared his throat. *Get back on your pony and ride, cowpoke,* he told himself. *Don't let this gal waylay you or your heart. You've got things to do that don't include the kind of life she's destined to lead.*

"What's so important your in-laws couldn't just send it in the regular mail?" he asked with forced casualness. He pointed to the pages pressed against the center of her lower lip.

"Oh, this?" She held out the white rectangle and stared at it. "Nothing earthshaking, I don't think."

"You don't *think*?"

"Yes. I, um—" She turned the papers over in her fingers, as if seeing them from every angle would somehow help her to make up her mind about them. "No, nothing too important. Important, yes, but not…"

"Not what?" he prompted.

"What, not what?" She whipped her head around to look at him, so fast that her blonde hair went swinging against her neck and cheek.

"Snap out of it, girl!" He stepped fully into the room, committing himself physically to an involvement he still wasn't sure he was mentally or emotionally ready to make.

But the protective beast in him had been stirred, and he couldn't walk away knowing Nina was in some kind of trouble—at least not without knowing what kind of trouble it was and if he could help. His gaze fell on the papers in her hands.

His gut instinct told him to take the letter and just read it for himself, but he'd seen Nina riled, and he figured grabbing that letter was a good way to get his hand slapped—or worse. He folded his arms over his chest and decided to try to cajole the information out of her.

"What was in that letter? Some kind of hypnotic suggestion?" He used the same soothing tone he'd use to coax a high-strung horse into cooperating.

"Hypnotic what? What are you talking about?"

"Well, you read it and suddenly you're in some kind of trance. I was thinking if it's that powerful, maybe you can loan it to me and I'll go read it aloud to that stubborn Shetland." His smile did not waver. "I confess, I wouldn't mind having that nasty critter under my spell."

"Well, now you've lost me completely." She shook her head. "One minute you're telling me to snap out of something, then you're rambling on about Plinkey and hypnotic spells."

The panicked twang edging her words told him she was more upset about the letter than she wanted to let on. He dropped the good-humored approach and opted for quiet, compassionate directness. "I see how this letter has affected you, Nina. I just wanted to know why and what I could do to help."

She clenched her jaw, turned her face away, then exhaled in one hard huff.

"If you must know, it was an invitation." She tossed the letter on top of the jumble of brochure samples, invoices, and cost estimates for a new generator that littered her desk.

"An invitation?" He pronounced every syllable hard against his lips and teeth. "To what?"

"The grand opening of Jackson's Butte Western Dude Ranch."

That was all? Relief flooded through him. He let a lazy smile creep over his lips. "Nina, there's nothing grand about this

65

place, but even so, why would your in-laws invite you to the opening of your own ranch?"

"They didn't invite me, they invited themselves." She raised her gaze to him, her expression filled with impatience.

"They sent a certified letter for that?" He sounded like he believed he was being lied to, or at least being kept in the dark about the details. He hadn't meant it that way, but there was no mistaking the challenging timbre in his tone.

"They sent it certified because they think it's so backward and isolated out here that anything less would be delivered by a broken-down pony express rider." She smiled, but her eyes told him she didn't find it funny. "And they wanted to make absolutely certain that I understood when they would be arriving and how long they would stay."

"And?"

She glanced up at him, and for the first time in this discussion, her eyes were focused. "And they told me exactly what they expected to find when they got here."

There was no place in the closet-sized room for him to sit. No place for him to pace. No place for him to even hang his hat on the goldenrod-colored wall. He narrowed his eyes and sighed, peering out the huge arched window that took up most of the wall space.

"What do they say they expect to find?" he asked quietly.

"More than I can provide in my wildest dreams, I'm afraid."

"I hired you to whip the ranch into shape, Clint, not me."

"Just hang tight to your clipboard, ma'am, and try to keep up with me." He strode through the swinging doors of the dining room, stopping to hold back one door so it wouldn't rebound and whack her in the nose.

Nina whisked past him, determined to do more than merely

"keep up" with the ranch foreman. This was her ranch, her dream, her future. This man may be the expert, but she was, and would always be, the boss.

"I'm just saying I think we can handle this work at a more reasonable pace. You're my ranch foreman, after all, not my personal trainer." There, that should clarify things quite nicely.

"A little hard work and hustle never hurt anyone," he countered. "In fact, it might do you some good."

She whirled around on her heel to confront him. "Are you saying I'm soft?"

Something peculiar crossed his expression, then faded. He released the door suddenly and it sprang back, then wavered a few times with a quiet creaking that reverberated in the empty room.

He cleared his throat and jabbed his finger toward the legal pad and clipboard in her hands. "If we're going to take an honest overview of what we need to do around this place, I think we should start at the same place they do—the front gates."

She planted her tennis shoes shoulder-width apart on the pine floor of the dining room, tucking the clipboard under her arm. "And I think we should start here in the main building and then go on to the guest cabins."

"Rather work inside, eh?" His accusation, couched in genuine humor, needled her already taut nerves.

He did think she was soft, she realized. Well, she may be a tenderfoot, but she was certainly not soft—not when it came to her business. Where that was concerned she could be every bit as hardheaded as that infuriating man—more so, if she put her mind to it.

"I'd rather work on what matters," she said in a deceptively calm voice. "If my guests aren't well fed and rested, if their showers clog or their mattresses are lumpy, they won't care one bit about the exterior trappings."

"They may not care, but what about your in-laws?" His tone mimicked hers. "I thought we agreed we needed to dazzle them from their very first sight of the place."

"We agreed to no such thing." She straightened her back until she felt the muscles tighten all the way down through her legs. "I'm not going to concentrate on superficial upgrades to try to fool my in-laws into thinking this pit is a peach."

"I'm not saying you should try to fool anyone, just that you need to add some eye-catching details." He shifted his weight off his bad leg. "Think of it as painting your front door before you put your house up for sale."

"I'm not selling anything."

"Oh yes, you are." He stuck his hand up and held up a finger for each point he made. "You're selling yourself, you're selling your vision for this place, you're selling your in-laws on the notion that they've made a worthwhile investment. That's what business is all about, lady—salesmanship."

"Salesmanship, maybe, but not false advertising. I won't work to perpetuate a lie all week, then polish up my halo and scoot off to church each Sunday." She folded her arms in front of her, clasping the stiff brown clipboard over her chest as if physically trying to hold in the flood of angry fear Clint's observations unleashed in her. "Besides, what happened to Mr. Let's-stick-to-the-basics?"

"You can't get anymore 'basic' than saving the ranch." He heaved a battle-weary sigh and paced a few steps away from her. "And I'm not telling you to lie. I'm telling you what needs to be done to make the best first impression on the people who hold the purse strings, Nina."

The people who hold the purse strings. The words settled over her like a heavy yoke. The none-too-subtle reminder of her indebtedness to the very people she'd sought to back away from created a sour, anxious churning in Nina's stomach.

The sick feeling gave a fierceness to the toss of her head as she answered in a thin voice, "This ranch cannot be geared entirely towards pleasing Mr. and Mrs. Jackson."

Clint halted in his tracks and twisted his head to peer at her over his shoulder. "Sounds like we're talking about more than the ranch, here, Nina."

She pressed her thumbnail to her lower lip then quickly pulled her hand away. She refused to dignify the man's nosy suppositions with an answer.

He waited, his eyes narrowed into near slits.

She swallowed hard, her lips sealed.

Something between a snort and a chuckle came from his lips. "Either way, there's plenty of work that needs doing before your in-laws—and your paying customers—arrive."

"Now, there's something that we finally agree on."

"We've got to get things organized, make a list of jobs, assign staff to tackle them—"

"Absolutely. I couldn't agree more."

"And if we're going to get that done in a timely manner, somebody has to be in charge," he said.

"And that someone is me!" they said in unison.

"The key to working on a ranch is trust and cooperation." Nina put her hand out to guide Alex as they walked toward the neat little row of guest cabins. "Everyone has a duty, and we have to be able to trust them to do it."

Once again she'd spouted a truth that, as a parent, she wanted her son to embrace. She wanted Alex to learn to trust the people he worked with, and to be worthy of their trust in return. Unfortunately, she wasn't being a very good example. *Do as I say, not as I do.*

Nina's stomach clenched. She did want to trust Clint

Cooper, but she just wasn't ready to do it. Not yet.

"Our duty today," she went on, "is to inspect each and every guest cabin to see what can be cleaned up and what must be replaced."

"I wanted to go with Clint to work on clearing out the riding paths." Alex stubbed the toe of his sneaker in the dirt. "Not poke through some ol' cabins."

Nina recalled Clint's jest about always having Alex underfoot and debated for a moment whether to explain to Alex that he was becoming a pest to the cowboy he so admired. One look in her son's shining eyes ended the debate.

"I understand how you feel, Alex. But the thing is, I really need your help, and Clint doesn't."

"You do? He doesn't?" The boy's eyes widened, as if both possibilities were equally baffling to him. He stopped in his tracks a few feet from the first of the boxy, wood-shingled guest units.

"Think about it," she urged, stopping as well. "Clint has four strapping young men to help him on those hot, overgrown, boring paths. I, on the other hand, have only you to help me tackle the mysteries of the many cabins." Her voice lowered as she spoke the last few words.

"The mysteries of the many cabins," he echoed.

Nina bent down to whisper into her son's ear. "Who knows what lurks behind those cabin doors, where no human has been for almost a year?"

"Wow." He mouthed the word. "What do you think we'll find?"

"Webs."

"Webs?" He scowled. "You mean huge, sticky webs from giant, icky spiders like this?" He bared his teeth and flapped his arms.

Nina smiled. "Probably not. The exterminators have been

through, and there are no more spiders, scorpions, snakes, or mice."

"Oh." The boy genuinely seemed disappointed. He gazed at some point around the toes of his shoes.

"However, I wouldn't be surprised if we did run into—"

His head jerked up.

She leaned in, as if sharing a special confidence. She wet her lips and pronounced each word in a whisper. "Great, big, giant, quivering—"

"What? What?" His legs jiggled in anticipation.

"Dust bunnies."

"Aw, Mama."

"I know it isn't glamorous work, or even fun, but that's the point I wanted to make about ranch life, Alex." She stood and fumbled with the dingy brass keys on the plain ring in her hand. "Everybody has their duty and everybody has to perform it because we all count on each other to keep the place running smoothly."

"Why couldn't my duty be with Clint?"

"Because working in the hot sun with weed cutters and shovels and chain saws all around is not a fit assignment for a little boy."

Alex opened his mouth to protest her verdict.

"And that's final," Nina said with a terse nod. "Our job today is checking out the cabins, understood?"

"Yes, ma'am."

Ma'am. Nina couldn't help smiling at Clint's influence there. She reached out and ruffled Alex's blond hair. "And we're going to do the very best job possible, right?"

"Right." His answer may not have been enthusiastic, but it was loud. That had to count for something.

"And nothing is going to get in the way of our doing our part, right?"

"Uh-huh."

"So when Clint Cooper comes home tonight, he'll take one look at our hard work and be so totally amazed, he'll have to admit that I—I mean *we*—know exactly what we're doing."

The very mention of Clint's name perked Alex up.

"Yeah." He swung a small fist in the air to show his eagerness to impress Clint.

Much as she hated to admit it, the idea that they were out to prove something to that bullheaded cowboy put a spring in Nina's step, too, as they resumed their walk toward the cabins. She'd show him that she was not just a greenhorn with a dream, a prayer, and a bankroll. She was a willing participant in the everyday chores of shaping up this ranch, as well as in running it.

"We are going to knuckle down, Alex, and tackle this job like real-life ranchers." Their shoes shuffled over the wooden sidewalk that ran in front of the row of cabins. "With skill."

"Skill," Alex echoed.

"And spirit."

"Yeah, spirit." He puffed up his little chest.

"With gusto."

"Gusto," he said loud and clear.

She halted outside the first cabin door. "And with a straightforward determination to do our best no matter how long it takes or how menial the task."

Alex blinked up at her.

She smiled weakly at him to apologize for getting carried away.

"And gusto!" he finally concluded in a deep, definite tone.

Nina jabbed a key into the lock on the first of the guest cabins. She pushed the door open. Cool, dark air and a gritty waft of dust greeted them. She switched on the light and the room filled with a yellow glow that did not quite reach into the corners along the back wall.

The woodwork was…well, rustic was a euphemistic term for it. The true color of the walls was indistinguishable in the faint light. The sparse furniture stood blanketed by so much dust she could barely identify each piece, let alone see what kind of condition it was in. The hardwood floors gleamed from some kind of coating that was slightly sticky underfoot.

Suddenly Clint's doomsday outlook seemed positively optimistic. Nina drew in a quick breath. Her nose tingled for a moment, followed by three abrupt sneezes.

"God bless you, Mama," Alex murmured.

"Thank you, sweetie." She brushed her knuckle over her son's cheek. "I needed that—in more ways than one."

God had blessed her, and despite what she now saw, his goodness surrounded her. She mustn't forget that, even as she tackled the monumental task ahead. She had an obligation to God as well as to her ranch and her family—to be a good steward and to maintain her attitude of gratitude.

A good lesson for herself and to share with her son, she decided.

"You know, Alex, just as all of us on the ranch are responsible to each other to do a good job and not to shirk our duties, we have another responsibility as well. Do you know what that is?"

The boy shook his head.

"To appreciate our blessings. And to remember to thank God for all he's given us."

"I'll remember, Mama." The sincerity in his eyes confirmed that he would indeed. "I have a lot to say thank you for."

"We both do," she murmured, her hand caressing his chin.

"Especially now that God has sent me my very own daddy to take care of us and the ranch."

"Not that again." Nina groaned, her hand falling away to slap against her leg. "Alex, honey, how many times do I have to go over this? God didn't send Clint Cooper to become your daddy. I hired him to be our ranch consultant. Can't you understand that?"

His pale eyebrows crimped down over narrowed eyes. "You mean you're the boss?"

"Yes!" Finally, he seemed to grasp it.

"And God's not?"

"No! I mean yes." She drew in a long breath of stale air and dust, sneezed once more, then hacked out a hard, dry cough. "Yes, God is ultimately the boss. Let's get to work, Alex, and I'll see if I can think of a way to explain this—again."

Nina sighed and walked toward the heavy lined drapes. She gave the twisted cord a yank, and the curtains lurched open with the screech of metal rings jerking over a metal rod. The sun streamed through in a dust-filled shaft of light.

"Look, Mom. Angels have been here."

Nina smiled at the idea that Alex had concocted as a tiny child—that the swirling particles glinting in the sunlight were evidence of angels' visits. Not a sound theological concept, she realized, but an endearing notion nonetheless. She believed it an expression of Alex's childlike faith. The very faith she was trying to nurture, not crush, as she struggled to sort out this matter of her son's claims about Clint Cooper.

"Oh, sweetie, what am I going to do with you?" She curled her fingers around the plastic tube at the end of the curtain cord. "I'm beginning to think my life would have been much less complicated if I'd bought a worm farm instead of a dude ranch."

"You'll get no argument from me on that one, boss lady."

At the sound of Clint's deep voice, Nina tensed, pulling downward on the aged cord in her grip. It snapped in her hand. She pivoted to face the man filling up the open doorway. "What are you doing here? Aren't you supposed to be clearing riding paths today?"

"I've got the boys working on them, but there's something

else that demands my attention right now."

Nina nipped at the side of her thumbnail. "Why do I feel like I'm about to get some really bad news?"

A slow smile inched over Clint's mouth. "It's not the news, ma'am, that's bad. It's the weather forecast."

"The weather?" She shook her head to show her lack of comprehension.

"Another spring storm's moving in late tonight." He jerked his head in the direction of the increasingly fierce wind. "If we don't want a repeat of the night we met, we've got to go pick up a generator and get it installed pronto."

"Today? But we have so many other things to get done." She glanced around the dingy room, then turned to look out the window. "Besides, the weathermen have been wrong a time or two. It certainly doesn't look like rain."

"Well, it feels like it." He hooked his thumbs in his waistband and cocked his hip, angling his weight off his bad leg.

She tried to come up with a joke about using the man's aching injury as an indicator of impending weather, but she could tell by the hard set of his jaw that he wasn't kidding.

"Anyway, after our talk this morning about who's in charge, I thought you might want to be in on the purchase."

"Because I'm in charge." She said it as a statement rather than a question.

"Because you have to write the check," he corrected. "But if you don't feel like tagging along—" He spun around on his boot heel and stepped out onto the wooden sidewalk, calling back, "I can always just have them send the bill to you."

"Let me find someone to watch Alex and I'll be right there." She grabbed Alex by the arm.

"But I thought it was our duty to inspect the cabins, Mama," Alex protested as he tugged his wrist from her grasp. "You said the key to running a ranch was to do your job and

75

trust everyone else to do theirs."

"Pretty sound advice, ma'am." Clint dipped the front of his hat downward as the hint of a smile played on his lips.

She couldn't help smiling back at him.

Then he had to add, "For a greenhorn."

Her smile pressed down into a scowl. "It doesn't take being an old cowhand to know how to live one's life or the right way to approach one's work, Clint Cooper. Those lessons come from another source."

"The Bible," said Alex in a helpful tone.

"And from the example of those who believe the Bible," Clint said softly.

That stung. The truth usually did. She had to be more than a lecturer to her son. She had to set the right example. She scraped her fingernail along the center of her lower lip, a fluttering heaviness in her chest.

"Don't you trust Clint to do his job while we do ours?" Alex gazed up at her.

Not yet. Her thoughts from a few minutes ago slammed against the reality of her present situation. Did she follow her anxious desire to see the ranch designed in her ideal, rather than Clint Cooper's? Or did she set the kind of example her son needed to see to become a godly man? She ground her teeth, knowing what the right answer was.

"Go ahead, Clint, get the generator. By the time you get back, Alex and I will have taken a thorough inventory of these cabins, and we'll have some idea where to start work tomorrow morning."

Chapter FIVE

I wish the electricity would go out all the time," Alex said, sitting cross-legged on the floor beside the stone hearth in the lobby.

Clint watched as the boy held out a hot-dog bun to take the blackened frankfurter Nina had prepared over the fire.

A hard rain pounded on the roof overhead. The wind whistled around the corners of the building. The electricity had gone out with the first few strong gusts of wind preceding the deluge.

"Well, if our Mr. Cooper keeps on spending as extravagantly as he did this afternoon, you may get your wish." Nina poked another frankfurter onto a stick and held it over the flames. "We may have to make do without some of the little luxuries—like electricity—permanently."

Clint clamped his jaw down hard at her words. He had been unable to arrange for the installment of the new generator soon enough to help them tonight. Now, Nina's gentle accusation made him wonder if he should have the equipment installed at all.

He leaned back, resting his palms against the rug. The firelight washed the room with a warm glow that made Nina's and Alex's hair shine like white gold, and the flames were reflected in the depths of their bright eyes.

His throat tightened. Of course he would have the generator installed. And he wouldn't allow himself to feel guilty for it, either.

"It's true, Nina. I went top drawer all the way on the generator and supplies." He narrowed one eye to gaze into the flickering fire. "And I won't apologize for doing it. This place isn't just a seasonal setup. You and Alex figure to make this your home year-round, right?"

"That's the plan, yes."

"Well, that means that once the summer, the guests, the staff, and, yes, even this good ol' cowboy are gone, you'll be out here all alone."

Alex, even though he had just taken a large bite of hot dog, opened his mouth as if to contradict Clint's assessment.

Nina held one finger up and shook her head at her son, then withdrew the frankfurter she'd been roasting and placed it in a bun for herself.

The boy shut his mouth and chewed in silence, with only the wrinkling of his nose to show his unhappiness with her intervention.

It tugged at Clint's battered heart to witness the interplay between mother and child. He swallowed hard to chase down the lump rising in his throat, just as he mentally forced down the unwelcome image looming in his mind of the wife and child long lost to him. He fixed his gaze on the little blond boy beside him and smiled.

Alex was a good kid, a great kid, a kid Clint couldn't leave out in the middle of nowhere without every support system necessary. "I did spend more than expected today, but I felt I had to."

Nina lifted a small mustard bottle, gave it a shake, then squeezed. A loud *braap* resounded in the quiet, as if Nina had stuck her tongue out at him. He was sure she wanted to.

The muscles between Clint's shoulders tensed. The fire popped and hissed. He would not be goaded into guilt about this, Clint told himself. Guilt led to justifications, and justifications meant having to face up to a few things that Clint wasn't about to confront just now. Maybe never. He'd done what he'd done based on good solid reasoning; surely Nina could understand that.

He glanced over at the firelight on her hair, her sparkling eyes, the expectant way she watched him and waited. The woman had placed her faith in God, then pinned her hopes on this busted-up cowboy. No matter that he was right; somehow Clint felt his solid reasoning didn't stand a chance against Nina's hopes.

He ran one hand back through his hair and sighed. "Nina, think about this a minute. I couldn't, in good conscience, leave you two out here with anything but the best, the most dependable, the easiest to run and maintain generator available. Top drawer."

"Which meant spending top dollar," she said, a sharp edge to her voice.

Clint drew in the aroma of the burning wood and the sizzling hot dog and held it. He turned his narrowed gaze on Nina. The fact that his selection might challenge Nina's budget had never occurred to him when he'd made the purchase. Of course, that was before he'd come home to her gloomy assessment of how much it would take to get the guest units whipped into shape. And the need to put the best face on things for the sake of her in-laws would certainly put a big dent in her resources, as well.

If she had promoted the place as rustic and the guests made

their reservations forewarned, she could have postponed some superficial things in favor of sinking her money into the essentials. But now she had to do it all: the little touches that would impress the people who funded her dream, and the larger investments he would not allow her to wait on.

"Yes, buying the best meant spending top dollar—but you make it sound like I squandered your last dime, Nina." He shifted his weight to relieve some of the ache in the leg stretched out before him on the hard floor. "Now, I understand your need to keep careful watch over your money, but there are some things you just can't afford to skimp on."

"And there are some things I can't afford at all," she said. Her eyes flickered over to Alex to indicate she would say no more in front of her son, then honed in on him to leave no doubt that he was one of the costly things she might have to do without.

The rain thrummed a steady rhythm overhead. Clint wanted to tear his gaze away from Nina's but he couldn't, no more than he could turn his back on her now that he'd gotten to know her and her son and the depths of their need. No matter what the personal cost, he decided then and there that he would pay them.

He leaned forward to pick up the poker beside the hearth. "Storm came up faster than I thought it would, son. But I promise, when we get that new generator installed, you won't be without electricity again."

Outside the wind blew hard against the windows and glass doors.

"In fact, son, with my help, you and your mama won't do without anything that's needed around here. You can count on that."

~ ~ ~ ~ ~

"How could you do that?" Nina marched back into the firelit lobby after tucking Alex in bed. She had steeled her resolve to do whatever necessary, including firing Clint Cooper, to save her ranch and her child's future.

"Do what?" Clint looked up from his seat on the floor, his back against the raised stone hearth.

"Make promises to Alex neither of us has any way of keeping, that's what." She could feel the tears threatening just below the surface, taste their bitterness in the back of her throat. She was afraid she wouldn't be able to maintain her cool facade much longer.

He lowered his gaze, which gave his eyes a smoky hooded appearance. His voice, quiet and controlled, fit his sober expression when he said, "I'm not a particularly religious man, ma'am. Not like you and the boy. I haven't seen the inside of a church in…a long time. But I know right from wrong. And I know Jesus put a lot of stock in caring for and earning the trust of children. I would never have promised the boy—or you—something I wouldn't try to fulfill to the best of my ability."

His confession and commitment touched her, but they did not alter the reality of her situation. "It's not your ability I'm worried about, Clint. It's mine."

"Yours?"

She moved over to the open area in front of the fireplace, then lowered herself to a cross-legged position on the braided rug. "Clint, I simply can't afford all the things you've promised."

"You're that low on funds." The words weren't spoken as a question.

"Oh, I could cover the costs today if I had to—but what about tomorrow?" She tucked her hands around her ankles, her shoulders slouching forward just a bit. "I have to think of making payroll, of covering bills, of making sure I can care for Alex for as long as it takes to get this place financially solvent."

"Of course you do."

"And that means exercising caution where spending money is concerned, perhaps even cutting out anything that isn't absolutely necessary."

"Anything, or anyone?"

She could not look at him.

"I see."

"I don't want to have to let you go, Clint. But right now you are my highest expense."

"Because of my salary or because I won't let you cut corners on things like the generator?"

She hunched forward even farther, drumming her fingers over the thick rug.

"Don't be afraid to be blunt, Nina. You won't hurt my feelings."

She lifted her chin high and narrowed her eyes at him. "All right, then, I will be blunt. When I hired you, I didn't balk at your asking price—because I thought you would save me money in the long run. That isn't proving to be the case."

He crossed his arms over his solid chest but said nothing.

"So far—" She raised one hand and began ticking off on her fingers the points of her argument. "You've caused me to totally revamp my menu, which did not come cheap. You cut down my number of riding trails significantly, hindering extra income from that, not to mention completely writing off any rental income from the mountain cabins this season."

"That was just common safety sense, Ni—"

She continued on to the next point, disregarding his argument. "You've said no to updated brochures and to expanding the dining room facilities, both of which might have brought in local customers and tourists interested in an evening meal."

"That would cost more than it would ever bring in," he grumbled.

She held up her thumb and pressed a finger to it to sum up her list. "And now to top it all off, you've purchased a generator at almost twice the price I'd budgeted."

He sighed.

"In conclusion, Clint, if there is anything I can't afford around this place—it's you."

"Nina, you're one smart business lady." He dipped his head in appreciation.

"I'm glad you feel that way, even after—"

"And you're a good mother, a fair boss, and a hard worker to boot."

"Well, I—" She ducked her head, hoping he'd think the warmth in her cheeks came from the radiant fire and not his glowing praise.

He raised one knee and rested one arm on it, his hand dangling down as he focused his cool gaze fully on her.

She braced herself for more compliments, feeling uncomfortable accepting them when she still planned to fire the man giving them.

"Really, Clint, please don't feel you have to say those things."

"Why not? They're true, every last one of them. And this is true as well—"

"Please, don't—"

"You are one lousy ranch foreman."

"Wh-what?" She blinked at him.

"No offense in that, of course."

"None taken, I don't think." She drew up her knees and looped her arms over them. "But I think I may have missed your point."

"My point is, Nina, that nothing in your experience gives you the skills to run a real ranch—even if it is just a dude ranch."

"It's business, isn't it?" she argued. "You yourself just said I was a smart businesswoman."

"Okay, smart businesswoman, what do you know about the care and feeding of your horses? And what about the kind of tack you're going to need?"

"Tack?" she whispered. While she recognized the term as meaning the horses' riding gear, she didn't know there were various kinds. Obviously Clint now knew it, too.

He shifted on the hard floor. "And what about handling the staff?"

"My staff?"

"You've hired some good kids, every one of them a sharp, decent, hard worker. But throw that many eighteen- to twenty-five-year-olds together for long periods of time, for an entire summer in an isolated ranch setting, and that's a recipe for mischief."

"Oh!" She put her hand to her throat, a sudden rush of modesty sweeping over her as she imagined the kind of situations she had, in innocence and single-mindedness over getting the ranch going, never anticipated. "B-but, I tried to pick kids who said they were churchgoers."

"I see."

Her throat constricted and her cheeks singed with the heat of her embarrassment as she continued to blabber, despite the knowledge that she should shut her mouth. "And—and I told them I had certain moral expectations, of course. But I didn't give it much thought beyond that, that's true."

"I didn't necessarily mean they'd get too friendly." He cocked his head and smiled. "I just meant that you'd have young men inclined to show off for the gals, maybe get reckless. Might even see a few fights. The kind of thing a woman like you wouldn't be able to keep under control the way an old hand like me would."

"Are you saying I'm not capable? That I need a man to step in and take charge?"

"For some things, yes." He crossed his arms and leaned back, the firelight gleaming in his hair. "Why, look at you, ma'am. You got all flustered at the very notion. I can't imagine you storming into a bunkhouse and riding herd on a bunch of young bucks all by your lonesome. But as for the gals—"

"Oh, I see. I need you to handle the animals, ranch operations, and the male staffers."

"And maybe a rowdy customer now and then."

What arrogance. Nina rolled her eyes at the man's old-fashioned cowboy code. Suddenly, she realized, she didn't feel so bad about having to let him go. It might teach him a much-needed lesson in humility as well as give her extra motivation to make this ranch succeed without his interference.

"And I'll take care of the girls and decorating the cabins and—"

"Now you're getting it. See how well we'd work together?"

"No."

"No?"

"The only thing I see, Mr. Cooper, is a man trying to justify my keeping him on when all reason points to the fact that I can't afford him."

"You can't afford not to, lady. Haven't you been listening?"

"Haven't you been listening? I can't continue to pay your salary and run the ranch according to your edicts." She punctuated her claim with a brisk nod. "But perhaps we can compromise. Now, if you'll agree to take back that generator and get an economy model and help me open up the mountain cabins, then maybe we can talk about finding a way to save your job."

"I'm talking about your only hope for saving the ranch."

"Which means having you as my foreman?"

"Yes, having me as your foreman—"

She clucked her tongue and shook her head.

He leaned in to command her full attention. "And as your partner."

"My what?"

"Partner. You know, as in throwing in an equal investment and getting half ownership in return?"

"You—you can afford that? Do you understand the kind of capital we're talking here?"

"Yep to both questions, ma'am." He nodded. "And then you won't have to pay me a salary or skimp on the necessities."

She narrowed her eyes. "And what do you get out of it, Clint Cooper?"

"It's a sound investment. I believe in it. And it would be nice to know I have my money working for me when I get back to the rodeo. And when I retire, I'll have a place to hang my hat—or if it's doing well enough, you can buy me out and I'll have the funds to do whatever it is I want then."

"And that's all you intend to get out of this?"

"That and a ten-gallon headache." He smiled and stuck out his right hand. "So, what do you say? Are we partners?"

She glanced at the callused hand of the man she'd come in here to fire, who was now offering to become her partner. She lifted her eyes to his. "Are you a Christian, Clint?"

He paused for a long moment before answering. "Yes, ma'am." A flash of pain so raw it made Nina glance away sparked in his eyes. "That is, I know the Lord and I love the Lord, but I don't think anyone would look to me as an example of Christ on earth, 'cause I'd make a poor, pitiful one, ma'am."

"Compared to the original, most of us do, Clint." Nina looked from Clint's offered hand to her own, lying in her lap. She'd asked God for help and each time help had arrived. Who was she to question what seemed like an answer to prayer?

A mother and a businesswoman, that's who. And there was

more to consider here than her immediate need. There was Alex, whose adoration of this man could be awkward at best. And there was the business, which she had hoped would be her very own, to provide for her son's present needs as well as for his future.

She glanced from her lap to Clint's steady and still-waiting hand, then to his face. Who was she kidding? There would be no business without Clint's help. As for Alex—despite his misplaced enthusiasm for a father, providing a kind, generous, hard-working Christian male role model for him wasn't exactly a lousy idea.

Nina didn't know which stuck out farther, her tentative hand or her pouting lip, when she sighed, cocked her head, and said, "You have a deal, Clint. Partners?"

"Partners."

"Just because Mr. Cooper is now temporarily a partner in Jackson's Butte Dude Ranch, does not mean that the chain of command around here has changed. I am still the primary owner, the one to come to with problems and for direction. I am the boss. Is that perfectly clear?"

"Uh, Mama?"

Nina lifted her brows as her son poked his head out from Plinkey's stall. "What is it, Alex?"

"Do you know that you're just talking to a bunch of horses' backsides?"

"And doing such a fine job, you'd swear she'd had a lot of practice doing that very thing." Clint strode into the barn, the sunlight behind him making him look like a walking shadow.

Nina flinched at being caught in the act of rehearsing the speech she was planning to make to the staff. Her cheeks flushed with warmth, and all she could think was that she must not get flustered. She had a right to make that kind of announcement to her staff. Still, it wasn't a subject she wanted to tangle over with Cooper just now. She seized on a welcome change of subject.

"You're an awfully brave man, Mr. Cooper," she said with a scowl.

"Brave?" He chuckled. "For what? Giving you such a good opening for an insult about your experiences talking to horses' behinds?"

"Actually, I meant for coming into the barn when your pal Plinkey is about to be let out to get some exercise." She moved stiffly to the front of Plinkey's stall, pretending that watching Alex tend his pony was the most fascinating thing on earth. "Or have you two settled your differences?"

Clint came up beside Nina. At that very moment, Plinkey decided to snort, while shaking his head so that the brunt of the watery blast covered the man's clean boots.

"Does that answer your question?"

Alex giggled at Clint's droll expression, then hung his head a bit to apologize. "Sorry about that, Clint. He didn't mean nothing by it, I'm sure."

"Don't worry about it, son. This ol' cowboy's gotten worse out of a pony and lived to tell about it." He smiled. "Now, let's see you cinch up your saddle nice and tight."

"Yes, sir." The boy nodded with enthusiasm as Clint stepped into the stall to lift the saddle.

"Here, let me get that." Nina stepped ahead of Clint to retrieve the saddle, feeling confident he had forgotten whatever he'd heard of her speech about remaining primary boss. "No sense pushing your luck around Plinkey any more than necessary."

Clint leaned in behind her so close that his words blew a strand of blonde hair to tickle her ear. "You're the boss."

She tensed, tightening her grip. The stitching in the smooth leather saddle chafed her fingertips. Clearly, her distraction ploy had failed. "So you heard that, did you?"

"What can I say? Face like a donkey and ears to match." He took the saddle from her hands and hefted it with ease onto the Shetland. "That's me."

"Oh, don't be silly." She reached over and adjusted the saddle just so on Plinkey's broad back. "Your ears aren't all that big."

He huffed, then shifted the saddle back again. "My ears are big enough to pick up on a load of nonsense when someone is spouting it."

"Nonsense?" She propped her palm against the saddle horn, ever so subtly nudging the saddle back to its proper place. "Nonsense? Since when has staying in control of one's business become nonsense?"

"When it stops being her business and becomes our business."

"It's my name on the ranch."

"And my money funding it."

"I have money in this, too."

"On loan."

"Some of it's my own. Not that that makes me any more or less of a partner."

"Finally something we agree on." He fixed the saddle firmly in the place he wanted it. "We're partners. That's what those papers said that we had drawn up this morning."

"Hey, you two. Cut it out."

Nina and Clint glanced down to see Alex wrestling with the cinch strap that they were jerking back and forth with each repositioning of the saddle.

"Maybe we should clear away from the pony and let the little guy do his job." Clint took her by the arm.

"My thoughts exactly." Nina yanked free of him and pushed ahead to lead the way out of the stall.

"You first, partner." He swept his arm out as if allowing her to pass.

"Don't mind if I do," she said, her smile too tense to be sincere. "Partner."

"Ah. Then you admit it."

"Admit what?"

"I am your partner."

"I know that."

"Well, you didn't sound like you knew it when you were addressing the stable a minute ago."

"I was just practicing how I would tell the staff about the changes. I don't see why it's such a big deal."

"You don't?" His eyes accused her of playing fast and loose with the truth. "Well, then, let's just take your speech and substitute my name in for yours and run that by the staff."

He had her there. She would no more like that than he liked being excluded from her vision of their working relationship. "Okay, okay. I get your point. However, to maintain order and get as much done as possible, I really think we need a centralized authority figure, Clint."

"Understood."

"And I think that should be…"

"Me," they said in unison. Nina frowned.

"Clint, it makes no sense for it to be you. When you leave to go back on the rodeo circuit, I'll be dealing with everything anyway. Why not start out that way and avoid confusion?"

"So basically, by becoming your partner I've been demoted from consultant to piggy bank."

She opened her mouth to say no, but she couldn't deny it. That was exactly what she was trying to do to him.

His gaze never left hers until he moved into the stall to

check Alex's work in saddling Plinkey. He crouched beside the boy, running his fingers along the latigo around the pony's round underside.

"Good job, son," Clint said in a gruff but quiet tone.

Alex beamed.

Nina felt ashamed of herself and the power struggle she'd been having with the man who had stepped in to help her out.

Clint stood slowly, favoring his bad leg, his hand on Alex's head in fatherlike approval.

Nina pursed her lips to say something; she wasn't sure what. But she knew she couldn't let this silence go on.

"Eeow!" Clint's hand slapped his leg.

Plinkey had struck again, taking a nip while Clint's back was turned.

"Why, you rotten little glue-factory candidate." Clint scowled as he rubbed his leg furiously.

"Did—did he hurt you?" Alex's face was white, his eyes enormous.

Clint turned, the sudden red of anger already fading in his cheek. "Just my pride, son. I should have known better than to turn my back on this critter. It's not like I didn't know the horse had it in for me, not something out of the blue from what I figured was a friendly source."

"Oh, all right." Nina shut her eyes so that she didn't have to see his expression when she caved in to his reasoning and not-so-subtle analogy. "You're an equal partner. When we tell the staff about the changes—together—I'll tell them that we both have equal authority over running the ranch."

Chapter SIX

What did Mama mean, Clint?"

Clint dragged his attention from Nina's starched posture as she walked away from their run-in, to Alex, standing on the other side of his saddled pony.

"What?"

"Mama said you'd be equal partners." The boy poked the toe of his tennis shoe into the stirrup and reached for the saddle horn at the same time.

In two long strides, Clint swept around Plinkey's head and gripped Alex under the arms. He lifted the small boy so that his foot fell from the stirrup. "Not that way, son. Always mount from the left side."

He set Alex's feet in the sweet-smelling straw and gave him an affectionate swat on the behind to send him scurrying around to the proper side. Clint watched the boy, ready to help out if needed but not wanting to steal Alex's chance to mount by himself. When Alex made the awkward climb and settled into the saddle, the smile he beamed at Clint rivaled the warmth of a fire on a snowy night.

"Good job, son." *Son.* For the first time, Clint choked on the word.

"Thanks."

Dad. The boy's lips hadn't said it, but his eyes had.

Clint tried to swallow, but a cold, hard lump held solid in his throat. He concentrated on the trivial details of adjusting Plinkey's bridle, but his thoughts were anything but trivial. The face of Mark, his own lost son, loomed large in his mind.

He'd thought he could control the obvious comparisons, thought he'd long ago conquered his emotions, strangled them into submission with an act of stubborn will. But looking into this boy's eyes had unleashed a flood of memories—good and bad—and the feelings that accompanied each of them. How long had it been since Clint had found himself dealing with so much emotion?

A dull, insistent pain swelled in his chest, and he wondered when he was ever going to be free from the guilt. Why had he put his career as a rodeo rider ahead of his marriage and family? Now, he had to live with his last images of his family: Jamie, eyes hot with anger, and Mark, his small face twisted in frightened tears. That wasn't the way he would have liked to remember them, if he'd had the choice.

Jamie had never been the type to give up on something she cared about. And neither was Nina. Clint tightened his jaw and forced back the instincts of fatherhood thrust upon him now. To protect and teach this child, to help him into a proper adulthood—those longings fought with the deeper and always fresh pain of regret in his heart.

Without thinking, he stepped back from the boy and let his hand drop from the horse's bridle. What he wanted now—what he needed—was distance. He needed to throw himself into this job, into allowing his leg to recover so that he could rejoin the rodeo circuit, and do whatever it took to avoid stirring up old feelings—or opening himself up to new ones.

"Clint?"

He started and looked up again at the boy, blinking to wash away his dismal thoughts and the image of his own son's face. "Hmm?"

"What did Mama mean when she said you'd be equal partners?"

"Um." Clint scoured his rough palm down over his mouth and chin and mumbled a noncommittal reply. "She meant neither one of us would be the main boss."

"So you're both gonna be servants then?"

Clint glanced up. That was strange wording for a child. His brows drew together and he tipped his head to one side. "No, we'll both be the bosses. Equal."

"In Sunday school they said we're all supposed to be servants. Didn't you ever go to Sunday school?"

Clint chuckled, a fragment of his humor returning. "Yes, I went to Sunday school a long time ago, when I was your age."

"Mama still goes to Sunday school, and she's a grown-up."

"That's good." He took Plinkey's bridle again and started to lead the pony out of his stall.

"Maybe you should go with us."

Clint heaved a world-weary sigh.

"I mean, if you and Mama are going to be partners, you should go to church with us. It says in the Bible you shouldn't be yoked to an unbeliever—that's like having Plinkey pull a wagon with a real big horse. It wouldn't work good."

"No, I guess it wouldn't, Alex, but—"

"You told Mama you want the ranch to work good. That's why you're helping, right?"

The kid had him there. What was that saying? Out of the mouths of babes... Clint nodded and stepped into the bright midday sunshine.

"Then you should go to church with us."

"I—I can't." He started to tack on the familiar "son," but it stuck in his clenched jaws and emphasized to him why he couldn't do as the boy asked. He could not allow himself to do anything to encourage any connections to this family. "I just can't."

"Why not?"

"Because," he snapped.

"Because why?"

"Just because, okay?"

"Because you want to be the boss and not the servant."

The child said it with a quiet, sad dignity that Clint could not ignore or dismiss. He'd never heard the truth spoken so bluntly yet so tenderly before. To think it came from the mouth of a seven-year-old boy. He doubted Alex even understood the depths of his insight into Clint's hardened character.

He wanted to be the boss, not just of the ranch, but of his life, of his feelings, of his past.

"My Mama has a poster on her wall with a Bible verse on it. Can I tell it to you?"

Clint swallowed hard, turned his gaze to the boy, and nodded in silence.

Pure concentration shone in the child's expression, as if he were picturing the poster. "It says 'Choose for yourselves this day whom you will serve.... But as for me and my household, we will serve the LORD.'" Alex looked up with a frown. "I can't remember what verse it is, though."

Choose. This day. The familiar words convicted him.

"Mama says that means that in our house, Jesus is the boss." Alex's face was solemn.

"No one can serve two masters." Clint murmured part of a verse from his long-ago church days. Which meant he couldn't call himself a Christian without surrendering his five-year service to his own guilt and remorse. He sighed. He'd been away from his faith too long. He hadn't abandoned it, but he sure hadn't done anything in a long time to nurture it. Well, he guessed he knew how to begin to change that.

He glanced up at Alex and mustered a determined smile. "Okay, little buddy, you win. I'll go to church with you and your mama next Sunday."

Nina studied Clint as he took Plinkey's reins to lead the pony with Alex on its back out into the open space between the barn and the main building. The man who had stepped in to help save a business that meant nothing to him was achingly gentle with the pony who would just as soon eat him as look at him. He held no malice or sought no revenge on the temperamental beast. He had asked no special favor for his help, either; just his due participation in the ranch operations—and even that wasn't for his own sake, but for Alex and her.

As Nina watched Clint guiding her son, kindness and patience toward the boy radiating from his ruggedly handsome face, she could think only one thing.

She had to get as far away from the man as possible.

Nina tucked her hands into her jeans pockets and sighed. Clint Cooper was working his way under her skin, and she could not afford that right now. What she needed was distance and time. She needed to get away to clear her mind and fortify her heart against the warm tenderness he inspired within her.

If they had met a few years from now, when the ranch was on its feet and Alex was less vulnerable to the damage of getting attached to someone who might not stay around, then maybe…

Maybe what? If Clint had not come when he had, there might not *be* any ranch. No, she told herself, God works in his own time and that had to be enough for her. Clint's arrival in her life now had been for the good and to wish for anything else was downright unappreciative.

Her best hope, her only realistic approach to handling her feelings and protecting Alex, was that they spend as little time alone with Clint as possible. From the corner of her eye, she saw Ellen striding toward them, a clipboard in her hand. Here came the perfect excuse to escape from Clint for the rest of the afternoon. Nina flagged the man and boy over with an energetic wave of her hand.

Clint handed the reins to Alex but kept a hand on Plinkey's bridle as they came toward Nina. Ellen reached her side just moments before Clint strolled up and opened his big mouth.

"Howdy, Ellen. You ready for a big announcement?"

The girl's eyebrows shot up. Her ponytail bounced from side to side as her gaze went from Clint to Nina and back again. "Announcement?"

"Now, Clint, this is hardly the time—"

"When better?" He chuckled. "We've reached a...mutually satisfying agreement, haven't we?"

Shock and almost devilish delight gleamed in Ellen's twinkling eyes at his words, but she said nothing.

Nina knew Clint didn't mean that as it sounded, but she felt helpless. There was nothing she could say to prove she and Clint had a strictly professional relationship without telling Ellen outright about the new partnership. She needed some precious time to collect her thoughts first. Besides, what Ellen knew, the whole staff knew; and that was not how Nina wanted to handle this.

"I plan on making a formal announcement at the morning staff meeting, Clint, no sooner."

"But I don't see why—"

"No sooner." Her jaws protested against the pressure of clamping them together.

She expected a protest. Instead she got a grin. A heart-stopping, we'll-do-it-your-way-this-time grin.

She swallowed hard to keep from sighing in response, then turned to Ellen. "Now that that's settled, is that the typed-up list of things we need for the cabin renovations?"

The girl pulled the clipboard from under her arm and held it out. "Yes, ma'am."

"Good." She took the list and began to study it. "Alex, you can ride a few more minutes, but then I'll need you to come shopping with me in town."

"Aw, Mom!" He jiggled his legs in a sudden jerking movement that would have been a foot stomping in other circumstances.

Plinkey lunged forward a step, but Clint held the animal in place.

"I only just got on." Alex stuck his lower lip out. "How am I supposed to learn to be a real cowboy if I never get to do anything but clean cabins and go shopping?"

"He makes a good point, Nina," Clint said in a soft tone that did not imply interfering. "I hadn't planned on hanging out with the half-pint, but I am going to be around this afternoon with no special plans. What say you go into town and I watch over the little guy?"

Nina blinked at the image of Clint with Alex. Mounted on the pony, the boy's anxious face was even with the big man's shoulder. The sight made her feel weak inside and her eyes watery, but that very response strengthened her resolve not to let this go on.

"No. Mr. Cooper has enough to do without adding baby-sitting to his list of responsibilities."

"But Mom—"

"It's okay, Nina, really."

"No, it's not okay, Clint. Really." She shook her head, telling herself she was doing what was best for Alex, keeping him from getting too attached to a father figure who had other plans. "I know Alex wants to learn to ride, and I want him to, but I just don't have the time for it right now."

"Fine. We'll take Plinkey back to the barn and then both be ready to go into town."

"Both?"

"Yeah, I'm going with you." It wasn't an offer, it was an edict.

"But what if I don't—"

"Mom, this isn't fair—"

"I thought we agreed, Nina—"

"Whoa!" For a petite girl, Ellen could make her voice heard when she wanted to. She held up both hands to halt the overlapping three-way argument in its tracks. "Hold it right there, ya'll."

"What is it, Ellen?" Nina folded the clipboard under her crossed arms, trying to look cooler than she felt.

"Well, I know I'm just a staffer here and it's not really any of my business, but I think I have the perfect solution to your situation."

"We're listening." Clint spoke for both of them and Nina threw him a sharp glance to let him know she did not appreciate it.

"Well, Alex wants to stay and ride, right?"

"Right!" Alex gave an enthusiastic reply.

"And you both want to go into town, right?"

"Right." Clint's reply rang with firm conviction.

Nina pressed her lips together in silence.

"And it's my job to stay here and tend to the horses anyway, right?"

Nina had to give a grudging nod, even though she could clearly see where the girl's logic was headed.

"Then why don't I take care of the horses and give Alex a riding lesson at the same time?" Ellen practically beamed. "Problem solved."

"Sounds good to me." Clint took the reins from Alex's small hands and started to give them to Ellen.

"Well, not to me." Nina intercepted the reins with a snap of the leather against her wrist. "It's not your job to baby-sit, either, Ellen."

"I don't mind, ma'am. Really I don't. And if it will give you two some time alone—"

"Maybe Mrs. Jackson thinks we've had enough time alone." Clint's quiet smile belied the heated words they'd just had. "And I can understand her position as a businesswoman and a parent. It's not fair for her to expect her staff to provide child care."

"Thank you, Clint." Finally, she might just get her way on something around here.

"I wouldn't have offered if I wasn't more than happy to watch over Alex, you know." Ellen sounded a bit wounded.

"'Course not." Clint gave the girl's shoulder a pat. "As I said, it isn't fair for Mrs. Jackson to put child-care duty on her staff—but since I'm not just staff anymore, it's perfectly fine for me to do it."

Ellen's posture perked up at Clint's insinuation.

Nina groaned inwardly, knowing the girl assumed that he and Nina shared much more than a working relationship.

"I'll stay with the half-pint, give him a riding lesson, and make sure he gets a good meal and is tucked in, so you won't have to rush home, Nina." Clint tugged at the reins, pulling the leather through Nina's fisted hand. But when the looped ends reached her, she held on. "You just take all the time you want and don't give us a second thought."

"Hooray!" Alex shouted. "I get to keep riding."

Nina shut her eyes to block out the temptation to say yes to Clint's generous offer. *Take all the time you want.* Time was, in fact, the one thing she did want. Time away from Clint, the very thing he was granting her.

Only one thing on earth could keep her from taking it. And that one thing was astride a fat, ornery pony, grinning his heart out at her. She would not sacrifice Alex's future happiness for a few hours of solitude. If she left her son alone now with Clint, it would give the child a chance to form a bond that would have to be broken. If she took the boy into town, Clint would surely come too, and she would run the same risk.

Clearly, there was only one thing for her to do, for Alex's sake.

"Ellen?" Nina lifted her chin and found her most sincere smile. "If you really don't mind taking care of Alex while Clint and I go into town—"

"Oh, not at all, ma'am. Not at all." The girl accepted the reins. "And just like Mr. Cooper said, feel free to stay in town for dinner and everything. I can stay until whenever you get home."

"Well, I don't think that will be—"

"Thank you, Ellen." Clint gave the girl a farewell nod, then took Nina by the arm. "We may just take you up on that."

Nina opened her mouth to make it crystal clear that they'd be home directly after the errands were run. She needed that stiff reminder as much as Ellen and Clint did, but she didn't get the chance to voice it.

"And as for you, little man." Clint aimed one narrowed eye at Alex. "You just remember that a real cowboy always minds his baby-sitter."

"Yes, sir."

A sudden choked laugh burst from Nina's lips. "If my experience with you is any indication, Clint Cooper, a real cowboy always *needs* a baby-sitter."

The cutting jibe meant to put emotional distance between them failed to do any such thing. Clint grinned down at her, draped his arm around her waist, and whispered in a voice far too intimate for casual conversation, "Then I guess I'm lucky to have you to look after me, aren't I?"

"No." Clint nabbed a packet of decorative brass nails from the orange basket on Nina's arm.

She continued to walk, moving down the aisle of the dusty hardware store, her back as straight as a board. Not even a hair on her head fluttered to indicate she'd turned to notice his actions. Clint quirked a tiny smile as he admired her self-control.

He hurriedly tossed the plastic box of nails back onto the metal shelf in approximately the right place, then moved along behind her again.

Nina reached for a packaged solid brass light switch cover dangling from a long hook.

Before her fingers closed on the cover, Clint cleared his throat.

Her shoulders tensing, she let out a short, irritated breath. But she skimmed past the solid brass fixtures and yanked at a brass-plated replica of her first choice. It landed with a clatter in the basket already weighted down with paintbrushes and masking tape.

Clint retrieved the switch cover and poked it back on a waiting hook even as she pulled free a second, then a third, and a fourth to plunk into her basket.

"No. No. And no." Clint snatched up her entire selection in one hand.

She snagged a handful of off-white plastic switch plates and threw them into the basket.

"Not even those." His hand dove in after them.

"Would you cut that out already?" She swirled around, her cheeks red and eyes blazing. "Don't you know it's rude to reach into a lady's shopping basket like that?"

"That so?" He hung the switch plates back, focusing on the task as though it were as delicate as disarming a bomb. "Where's that written?"

"It's not." He heard her move but did not look, assuming she'd resumed her furious march into bankruptcy as she mumbled just loud enough for him to hear, "It's an unwritten rule."

"In other words—" He turned to follow and found himself practically stumbling over her. He pulled up short but could not keep his chest from brushing against her arm and shoulder. He cleared his throat again. "In other words, you just made it up."

"I did not." She did not back down verbally or physically but stayed so near he could feel her annoyance in the steady rhythm of her breathing. "It's…it's just common courtesy, that's all."

Clint clamped his jaw tight. The smell of the old hardware store, of metal and wood and at least two generations of hard-earned grime, could not mask the subtle scent that wafted to his nose as Nina shook back her soft, shimmering blonde hair. He wanted to touch that hair, to pull the gal close and drown in the beckoning smell of lotions and powders and her own delicate skin. He wanted to kiss her.

He edged forward a shuffled half step. He could feel the warmth of her, see the pupils of her clear eyes grow larger with his encroaching nearness. He cocked his head and bent his neck to put his gaze inches above hers.

"Do you know what I consider a common courtesy?" he asked, his voice raspy from the strain of controlling his desire to hold her.

"What?" she whispered. Or had he just imagined he heard the word her lips formed?

Don't. Even as his fingers flexed, aching to reach for her, his mind gave out a strict warning. He'd known from day one that dealing with this pretty little streak of stubbornness in a woman's body would get him knee-deep in trouble. When he'd agreed to come on board as her partner in that last-chance dude ranch, he waded in hip-high. Then when he'd promised her son he'd start coming to church with them—he'd put himself in up to his chin. If he took her in his arms, told her of his attraction to her, of how she awakened things in him he'd thought gone for good, if he kissed her...

She blinked up at him, her thick lashes dipping to brush above the blush on her cheeks. Her teeth sank into her full lower lip.

His throat tightened around a lump that suddenly seemed a jagged ball of fire.

If he did that, he told himself, and she did anything but slap his foolish face and tell him to get in touch with reality, he'd be in over his head.

He blew out a ragged breath and stepped away from her. "I consider it a common courtesy not to allow a lady to fancy-gadget herself into financial ruin."

Her hands fell heavy at her sides. "You have got to be kidding."

Was it wishful thinking or did Clint see disappointment in Nina's eyes? Could she have savored their brief closeness as much as he had? Would she have welcomed more?

He'd never know now. She groaned out a sigh, spun on her heel and said, "You're trying to tell me that a few nails and some light switch covers are my ticket to the poorhouse?"

"'Take care of the pennies and the dollars take care of themselves'; that's my motto."

"Really?" She twisted her neck to glance at him with a raised eyebrow. "I figured your motto would be something like, 'my way or the highway' or to put that in cowboy speak, 'my trail or out on your tail.'"

He had to chuckle. Had to. Otherwise he'd respond to her sarcasm in kind and then where would they be? Not one step closer to accomplishing what he intended to accomplish by becoming her partner in the first place—getting her ranch set up proper.

"Okay," he admitted. "Maybe I have been a bit…forceful in presenting my solutions."

"A bit?" She shook her head as if trying to dislodge the understatement. "A *bit?*"

"Oh, come on. I haven't been all that bad, and if I have, I had my reasons."

"To drive me absolutely batty with your nit-picking?" she asked.

"No, to protect you from bad management decisions."

"Oh? Like the shocking madness of buying replacement plates for the cabin light switches?" She put her wrist to her forehead like some damsel in a silent movie. "Oh, thank you, kind sir, for saving me from my own extravagance."

"It is an extravagance, Nina. It's a waste of time and money, and we don't have either to spare." He took the shopping basket from her hand. "Paint is cheap and fast."

"Paint?" A small crinkle appeared between her eyebrows.

"Yes, paint." Clint could not look at her anymore without fearing his feelings might show through. He gripped the basket handle and headed up the aisle, making a beeline for the checkout counter. "We've got the hardware fellows loading gallons and gallons of sunset beige into my truck at this very moment, remember?"

She followed on his heels. "That paint is for the cabin walls."

"The walls, the furniture, the light switches."

"The—?" Her fingers curled into the fabric of his shirtsleeve. "You can't do that!"

Her gesture made him stop in his tracks, but when he spoke to her, he looked somewhere in the direction of the plumbing fixtures. "In a couple years when the ranch is a gold mine, we can—that is, *you* can gut the cabins and do them any way you want. For now, we paint."

"All sunset beige?" She sighed.

"Yep."

"Great." She shut her eyes. "Our guests will feel like they're living inside a great big egg."

Clint laughed. "It won't be so bad. You'll see. Everything will have a clean, fresh look, be easy to wipe down between occupancies, and you won't have to worry about matching the color scheme to every painting, fabric, and doodad you stick in there."

"My goodness, a rodeo cowboy with a sense of interior design." She offered a genuine smile that made her eyes shine with mischief. "Why didn't you put that on your job application?"

"Just so happens, I've been a landlord for a few years. Learned a thing or two about it in the process." He thought of the once-cozy home he'd shared with his wife and son that he'd been renting out for nearly five years.

He thought of the sunny kitchen where he'd last said goodbye to Jamie, his wife. He thought of the backyard with the tire swing and half-finished tree house that he'd torn down in rage after his son's death. He remembered how vast and empty that small place had seemed when filled to the rafters with his grief and loneliness. And his guilt.

Despite the new revelations during his talk with Alex, the old convictions haunted him with renewed harshness. Clint had himself to blame for the loss of his family. If not for his pig-headed selfishness, today that house would hold happy memories for him—and for his family.

That sentiment washed away any remnants of longing for Nina that lingered. Clint Cooper was not meant to be a husband and father, and he would never ask anyone—especially Nina and Alex—to suffer through his second attempt to prove otherwise.

"So you have rental property?" She leaned forward to take the shopping basket from him. Their fingers brushed, and as if she felt a jolt of electric shock, she looked up at him. Perhaps the coldness in his gaze told her not to push the subject, since she dropped her chin. "I didn't know that about you," she said softly.

His gaze fell to her mouth. He thought of how close he had come to kissing those lips, of how many times he'd let his attraction to her guide his judgment, of what a dangerous habit that could become for all of them. He pushed his fingers back through his hair and gave a one-sided, wincing smile. "You know, little lady, there's probably a whole world of things about me that you don't know."

And for all our sakes, you never will.

Chapter SEVEN

You're what?" Nina watched Clint cross the lobby, his usual jeans and western shirt traded for a simple but expensive dark suit and deep red tie. She hadn't spoken to him since their ill-fated trip to town the night before.

"I'm coming to church with you."

Nina shook her head, squinting into the blazing sunlight that streamed in through the glass doors and high windows. "I don't understand."

"Well, I know you go to church regularly. And I recall a discussion by the fire earlier this week when I told you I was a Christian myself." Clint's boots, a pair of highly polished black ones she'd not seen before, scuffed on the tile floor as he came to a stop. He ran the edge of his thumb along the rim of his black cowboy hat. "So, just what is it that has you so baffled, Nina?"

"Um, for starters, you don't even know which church we're going to," she argued lamely.

Why was he doing this? She suddenly felt as if she had no place of solace, nowhere to hide from this man and the feelings he evoked in her. Wasn't it enough that they would be spending most of their waking hours together going over books, meeting with staff, and doing whatever else it took to keep the ranch operating? Now she was expected to share her Sunday mornings with him as well?

She crossed her arms, disregarding the wrinkles it made in her simple pink dress. "I'm not questioning your going to church, Clint. I think you should."

"You mean you think I need it." His frown didn't mask his good humor at her expense.

"I think everyone needs it."

"But?"

"But why would you want to come to church with us?"

"Because I was invited, for starters."

"Invited? By whom—"

Alex burst into the room, his blond hair combed into uncharacteristic submission. He squirmed in his navy blue blazer, and the ends of his clip-on necktie flapped in salute as he beamed at them. "Hiya, Mama. Hi, Clint—are you ready to go to church with us?"

"Alex," she murmured. The picture fell neatly into place.

"Your son oh-so-wisely pointed out to me that if we were to be equal partners, I should be going to church, too." Clint pushed his open suit jacket back to tuck one hand in his pants pocket.

"He did?" Her cheek twitched as she tried to form a smile for her son. "You did?"

"Yeah, on account of the yoke." He nodded as if that made perfect sense.

"The...?" She looked to Clint, her smile a bit easier this time. "What? Are you finally doing penance for those awful fried eggs you've forced us to have on the menu?"

He chuckled.

"Not an egg yolk, Mama, a yoke—like on oxen."

"Oxen?" She drew in a deep breath and found it rich with Clint's aftershave. She exhaled in a whoosh and shook her head. "You mean like 'Ollie, Ollie, oxen free?'"

Clint groaned. "That's 'all the, all the outs in free.'"

"No, it's not," she protested. "Anyway, how would you know?"

"Mama." Alex tugged at her arm to pull her toward the front door.

"I know because I was a kid once." Clint stepped forward to grasp the doorknob, his long arm extending along her back. "I also happened to have played that game a lot with my—"

He cut himself off, but Nina saw a brief flash of intense pain in his eyes.

"I just know, that's all." Clint pulled open the door for her. "Point is, Alex wasn't talking about egg yolks or misquoted kiddie games. He was referring to a Bible lesson."

"Mama?" Alex tipped his head back.

"A Bible lesson?" She paused to snatch her purse and sling it over her shoulder.

"I looked up the verse after we talked about it. It's in Second Corinthians."

"What is?"

"'Do not be yoked together with unbelievers,'" Clint quoted.

"Oh. But how—"

"Mama?" Alex interrupted with a little more volume.

Nina sighed. "What is it, Alex?"

"Why don't animals go to church?"

"Oh, I don't know, Alex." She pressed her fingertips to her temples. "Because animals don't need to go to church."

"That's true, half-pint, animals don't need it. But those of us that do had better get moving or we'll be late." Clint checked his watch, then glanced quickly at Nina to ask silently if he would be welcome to join them.

"Oh, all right." She ushered Alex ahead with a firm hand on his back and as she brushed past Clint she managed a watery smile. "But I think we should take separate vehicles, and I don't think we should sit together. What with the two of us now co-owning the ranch and living out here under the same roof—"

"Half a building apart." He followed behind her and pulled the door shut with a bang.

"But under the same roof all the same." She straightened her shoulders.

She felt him reining in a grin at her modesty, but she didn't care.

"If we drive up together and sit in the same pew at church, it might give people entirely the wrong idea." She shook back her hair and tipped up her chin. "I have a reputation to protect, Clint, as a business owner, a mother, and a Christian. Not to mention how my in-laws might react if some ugly gossip got back to them while they're here."

"I think you're making a much bigger deal out of this than it warrants, Nina."

"You don't know how it can be, Clint. If we don't keep our distance, I can just imagine the kinds of things people might say."

"What a lovely couple!" Alex's Sunday-school teacher, a cherub-faced woman with silver blue hair and the best of intentions, cornered Nina and Clint after the service. Even though they hadn't sat directly next to each other during worship, when the service was over, they headed to the basement to collect Alex together. That's when it happened.

"We're not—"

"Actually, we're just—"

The woman swept their mutual objections aside with a wave of her hand. "I've seen Alex's mother in passing for several weeks, but never got the chance to talk with her. It's such a hectic time, you know, and today with all the folks coming for the choir competition this afternoon, it certainly isn't any quieter."

"Sure," Clint said, casting Nina a sympathetic wince.

She pursed her lips, and he braced himself for a staunch denial of their couplehood. But before Nina could voice a single objection, the teacher grabbed Clint's hand and gave it a vigorous shake.

"You must be so proud of Alex."

"Well, I—"

"He really takes to the lessons and participates. I hope it doesn't embarrass you if I say he talks about you a lot."

"He does?" Nina and Clint spoke at the same time.

"Oh, yes, it's always 'my dad this' and 'my dad that.'"

Clint felt Nina tense beside him as his own gut constricted.

"He says you've been on the rodeo circuit. I assumed that's why we never saw you before, but the moment I laid eyes on you, I knew you were Alex's father."

If this cheery Aunt Bea look-alike had just landed a sucker punch to his stomach, she could not have shocked him more. He struggled to take a breath. He didn't blame the woman—after all, she'd only been repeating what she'd been told—but he did feel the need to set her straight about him and Nina and Alex.

He lifted his gaze over the woman's fluffy hair and studied the boy, who was concentrating on putting away felt cutouts of Bible characters in a cardboard box. His son. If only that were true. If only that could ever be true.

Clint cleared his throat and found a gentle smile for the teacher. "I'm afraid you've made a—"

"Excuse me, please." Nina nudged past him, bumping against Clint's chest in her haste. As she slipped between them, he could see the red in her cheeks, hear the clipped urgency of her high heels on the tile floor.

"Nina, it's not a big deal," he said quietly, trying to snatch her by the arm as she brushed by. "He's just a kid, after all."

She twisted her head around, fire flashing in her eyes. "He's just a kid who was warned not to tell people that wild story about thinking you're his heaven-sent father."

"His—?"

"Did I say something wrong?" The teacher wrung her wrinkled hands.

"No, no, it's fine," he assured her, even as his mind whirred to process what Nina had just said.

"It's time to go, young man." Nina placed the box of felt pieces on the shelf and took Alex by the hand.

"Are we going to stay for the choir competition then go out to eat with Clint, like the other kids' families are doing?" His eyes were wide and so full of hope that Clint couldn't help but feel a twinge of regret that they wouldn't be doing just that.

"No, because we are not a family," Nina whispered. "That is, we are, but not Clint. I explained that to you before, didn't I?"

Alex nodded, his small mouth tugged down at the corners.

Clint stepped aside to allow the mother and son to move quickly through the doorway, then he gave the teacher a reassuring smile. In the hallway, a throng of church members, their children, and a single file line of teens in long purple choir robes, all heading in the opposite direction, trapped them in place for a moment.

Nina would not look at him, and Clint told himself that was probably for the best. He didn't know if he could meet her gaze just now without revealing too much of his turbulent emotions. Still, he was aware of her nearness and of her discomfort over Alex's tale-telling.

A woman with an armload of music all but spilling from a leather case balanced like a baby on her hip tried to squeeze by them. Nina stumbled a step to make way and landed the heel of her shoe right on Clint's toe.

Nina gasped. "Oh, I am so…"

He took her by the arms to steady her.

She tipped her head back, her gaze finding his. She wet her lips. "Sorry."

He gazed down at her face, and for a heartbeat the hustle around them was just a blur of noise and color.

"Excuse me, sugar." The harried choir director's voice cut through the moment. "It's just so crowded in here, and I need to get this music to our substitute organist—"

The woman moved on, caught up in the stream of purple robes.

"Clint, I'm sorry about the thing with Alex," Nina said as they inched forward.

"Let's not give it another thought." As if that were possible. He knew he'd never forget hearing himself called the boy's dad. "I know how kids are."

"You do?"

Yes, he did. But that wasn't something he wanted to go into now, perhaps not ever. He lifted his shoulders and let them fall as much to physically shrug away his thoughts as to appear unaffected by Alex's claims. "I know kids make things up. Say all kinds of things—especially things they know grown-ups want to hear."

"What grown-ups want to hear?" In the closeness of the hallway, he could feel her body stiffen. Her eyes narrowed and her jaw set. "Are you saying that I somehow put this idea in Alex's head? That he's going around saying you're his father because that's what I want?"

He opened his mouth to speak, but she did not give him the chance.

"Of all the egotistical, self-centered…I just have one thing to tell you, Mr. Clint Cooper."

He put a finger to his lips to try to get her to lower her voice.

"When I do decide to remarry and find a new father for my son, it certainly won't be with a man who is such a big-headed jerk that we could use his cowboy hat for a swimming pool." She spun on her heel, lifted Alex, and forged her way through the crowd.

Clint gave the group of wide-eyed listeners a sheepish grin, cleared his throat, and went after her. He didn't manage to catch up to her, but he did hear the last thing she told her son before they merged in with the others. "And on our way home, young man, you and I are going to have another long talk about this father by faith business."

Father by faith? The words crashed against Clint's heart like a wave. They brought him to a dead halt. Though he'd found today's sermon thought provoking and the music uplifting, the most profound thing he'd heard today might just be those three words.

Could it be that the Lord had brought Clint to this point in his life to become that very thing? A father, by virtue of a little boy's conviction and his own renewed faith? The idea humbled, frightened, and yet intrigued him.

The choir competitors and the church members headed for the fellowship area pressed around him in the narrow hallway while Nina pushed on ahead. For a moment more he could see the two blond heads, and then they disappeared into the stair-well.

He angled his shoulders to wedge his way against the flow of people and hurried through. But by the time he got to the parking lot, Nina was in her car and driving off. Driving off just a little too fast for common safety, he thought. The realization dropped like an icy rock in the pit of his stomach.

He wanted to go after her, to watch over her, to keep her from any harm her own haste and his careless attitude might have brought her. He wanted to do for Nina and Alex what he had not been able to do for his late wife and son: protect them.

He strode with a purposeful stride to his truck, yanked the door open, and got in. The engine revved to life and he threw the truck into reverse, laid his arm across the back of the seat, and twisted his head to check behind him. Just then, a bus carrying a visiting choir pulled in directly behind him—and parked.

"Don't you ever speed off in a huff like that again!" Clint burst into the cabin just as Nina raised the loaded paint roller.

Holding it aloft, she ignored the stream of paint trickling recklessly down the roller handle and blinked at the man.

"Well, don't you ever say 'don't you ever' to me in that tone of voice again," Nina shot back, defensive despite her confusion over Clint's outburst. If anything, she'd expected a confrontation about Alex's behavior, not her own.

She'd arrived home over thirty minutes ahead of Clint, time enough for Alex to race inside, change into play clothes, and dash out to the barn to share his Sunday-school lesson with Plinkey. She'd used that time to calm herself over the humiliating incident, convinced that after this last talk, Alex would not be proclaiming Clint Cooper as his father again. She'd changed into a ranch logo T-shirt and her most beat-up jeans, grabbed a couple of doughnuts from the continental breakfast tray provided for the staff, then headed for the only cabin still unpainted. She'd hoped that the hard work might take her mind off things—off Clint.

She'd just wanted one afternoon when she didn't work with Clint, talk to Clint, or even think of him. It stood to reason, of course, that he would seek her out immediately upon arriving home.

She stood there with her hair pulled into a lopsided ponytail on top of her head and sunset beige paint dripping onto her shoes and trickling in rivulets down to her elbow. Bits of chocolate doughnut crumbs clung to the front of her T-shirt and probably to her mouth as well. Still, she managed to respond in a dignified voice. "You may be my partner in business, Clint Cooper, but that does not give you the right to come storming in here and talk to me like I'm some kind of child."

"How else do you talk to someone who's acting like a child?" His pale lips set in an unyielding line, his face half in shadow beneath the brim of his deep black cowboy hat.

"I wasn't aware that I was acting like a child." She batted her lashes, placed the paint roller back in the pan, and wiped at the sweet bits of chocolate doughnut on her lips with the back of her hand. A damp stickiness spread after she pulled her hand away. She tipped her tongue out and cringed at the chalky bitterness she tasted on her lips.

She didn't need a mirror to tell her that she'd just smeared a nice fat blob of sunset beige over her mouth and cheek. She jerked her head up, determined to overcome her appearance with a calm resolve. "If you have a problem with my driving, I suggest you speak to me about it in a civilized manner. Or better yet, why don't you keep your opinions to yourself, as it's really none of your business."

"As far as you're concerned, not even my business is any of my business." He tipped his hat back. The sunshine from the open cabin door contrasted with his dark form, accentuating the width of his shoulders and the lean lines of his legs.

Nina cocked her head and felt her precarious sprout of a

ponytail bobble. "Your point being?"

"My point being that if I left everything to you, nothing short of how I dress would be my business."

"Says a man wearing his expensive dress clothes near wet paint."

"I would imagine I'm pretty safe from this distance." He folded his arms, half sneered a grin, and leaned back against the door frame.

"Clint, look out, there's fresh paint!"

"Wha—?" He jumped away, then nearly turned in a circle as he craned his neck to see his back.

Nina laughed aloud. "Made ya look!"

He shut his eyes and clenched his jaw.

She laughed harder.

When he opened his eyes, he shook his head. "Nina Jackson, I can't believe you lied just to make a fool out of me. And on a Sunday, too."

"I did not lie." Her protest was punctuated by a fading laugh. "All I said was 'look out, there's fresh paint.' And sure enough, here it is."

She reached over and took up the paint roller again, brandishing it high like Lady Liberty with her torch of freedom.

"You think you're pretty funny, don't you?" He cocked an eyebrow as he slipped his suit jacket from his shoulders.

She had no idea what he had in mind, but she knew she didn't want to stand there and wait to see what it was. "Stay where you are, pal."

He tossed his suit jacket over the nearby chair, took a step, then loosened his tie.

"I mean it." She lowered the paint roller to point it directly at him, only half teasing as she promised, "This thing is loaded, and I know how to use it."

She wasn't afraid of the man. If she wanted to admit it,

which she didn't, she was, in fact, more afraid of herself. If he crossed this room, sidled up as close to her as decency allowed, and looked into her eyes, as he had the last two times they'd stood toe-to-toe, she doubted if she could keep something from happening between them. Something she'd been fighting against since she first laid eyes on the cowboy.

"Ah, so you've graduated from textbooks to semigloss indoor latex."

She crooked a smile. "This happens to be high gloss, mister, so stand back."

He took another step and then another. "You wouldn't."

A thick dollop of pale paint plopped to the newspaper-covered floor. "I might."

"Well, I'm bettin' you won't." He tugged his hat off, threw it onto the canvas-covered dresser, and charged the last three steps.

He had his hand on the roller handle before Nina knew what had happened. The menacing paint roller left her palm, fit into his grasp, and then fit back into the paint pan in one smooth movement. Not without casualties, of course. Tiny droplets of pale sunset beige paint flecked the wall, the ladder, the drop cloth, and Nina's hair.

Clint, to her complete irritation, stayed as unmarred as a drift of fresh snow.

Her agitation lasted all of a split second as Clint's rumbling laughter tapped into her own sense of the ridiculous at their behavior. She let go with a hearty peal of laughter.

"I can't believe you pulled that off without a single splat of paint on you." She crinkled up her nose at him.

"You know what they say, lady." He sounded like Clint Eastwood and John Wayne rolled into one giant cornball.

"No, what do they say?"

"Only the good 'dye' young."

She shut her eyes.

"Get it? Dye, d-y-e?"

"Oh, I got it all right." She reached behind her back, her fingers wriggling to touch the roller again. "And just for that, you are going to get it."

"Oh, I don't think so." His hand closed over her arm and lowered it gently, bringing his body close to hers. "In fact, if anyone is going to get it, young lady—"

Suddenly she was in his arms. Her heartbeat thundered against his chest and her chin brushed the soft silk of his tie. She tipped her head back, both eyes fully open. What she found in his gaze made a gasp catch in the back of her throat.

"You really are going to get it," he whispered again.

She wet her lips. "You wouldn't."

He lowered his head. "I might."

"I'm betting you wo—"

His mouth came down over her lips.

Nina shuddered, her eyes fell shut, and she gave herself over to the kiss she'd both dreaded and desired.

It lasted far too long and it was way too brief. And when it was over, they pulled apart as if the contact had caught their shirtfronts on fire.

Nina backed away a step, her gaze sweeping the room. "That can never happen again," she announced, her voice breathless and strained. "And no one can ever know that it happened. No one. The staff is already treating us like we're a pair of star-crossed lovers; if they knew this…and Alex—" She groaned aloud. "Oh, no, that cannot happen again."

His hand swept back through his hair. "It never should have happened in the first place."

"Don't say it like that." She scowled in his general direction, unable to look directly at the man she'd just kissed.

"Like what?"

"Like it was…distasteful to you, or something." She folded her arms and dropped her gaze to the paint-spattered floor. "You liked it, Cooper, and you know you did."

"Oh? And you didn't?"

"No, I didn't." That was true in a certain sense; just not the sense he had meant. She did not like that she had allowed the kiss to happen, especially now. She did not like it at all. She jerked her chin up but still did not meet his gaze. "And as far as I'm concerned, you needn't worry about that ever happening again on my part."

He huffed out a one syllable laugh. "Good to know I can trust you."

She gritted her teeth. "I only wish I could say the same for you."

She heard him move seconds before she felt the warmth of his body pressing against her. His hand curved around her arm as he drew her up to him again. He commanded her gaze to meet his.

She swallowed hard and slowly raised her eyes.

"Now, you listen here, Nina. I've put up with your greenhorn bossiness, your trying to make me such a silent partner I'd be invisible, and your kid's daddy recruitment program."

She cringed but did not look away.

He raised his hand and shook one finger in warning. "But there's one thing I am not going to stand for—"

"Mama, can Ellen and I go riding—"

"Mrs. Jackson! Mr. Cooper!"

They turned to find Alex and Ellen standing in the doorway, bug eyed and mouths gaping.

Nina blinked.

Clint wagged his finger again, disregarding their audience, or perhaps for their benefit. "There's one thing I am not going to stand for, and that's you trying to paint this cabin by yourself."

"What?" She frowned in confusion.

"I'm going to get changed and get right back in here and help you." He cleared his throat and strode toward the door. He glanced at Alex and Ellen as he gathered his hat and jacket. "And as for the two of you, well, either you get in here and help us out, or you get out of the way."

"You mean we can go riding?" Suspicion colored the boy's question.

"Better that than underfoot around here. We've got a lot of work to do. Now get going."

Ellen stole a fleeting, amused look at Nina for her approval.

The nod and sheepish smile she gave must have done the trick, for the girl stifled a giggle, ducked her head, and nabbed Alex by the hand.

"C'mon, cowpoke, let's get Plinkey saddled up."

Alex rubbed the back of his hand over his mouth, his nose scrunched up. He kept his curious gaze focused on them, going from Nina, to Clint, then back to Nina, as Ellen tugged him outside.

The minute they had left the scene, Clint spun to face her. "Well?"

"Well, what?" she asked.

"Well, do you think they bought that?" He put his hands on his hips.

Nina rubbed a fingertip across her lip, pulled it away, and examined the whisper of paint there. Then she lifted her gaze to the bold streak of sunset beige across Clint's mouth.

She sighed, shook her head, and still managed to laugh as she admitted, "No, Clint, I don't think they bought it for one single, solitary moment."

Chapter EIGHT

Yes, yes. Thursday night. We'll be looking for you." Nina shifted her shoulder to ease the crick in her neck. The telephone receiver almost slipped from its perch beneath her chin, but she caught it without missing so much as a beat in the conversation with her mother-in-law. "Uh-huh. Oh, yes, I don't think pleasantly surprised would be an overstatement. In fact, I'm sure you'll be very pleased. Okay. Bye now. Yes. Bye. Um-hmm. Bye-bye. Bye. Good-bye."

"Oooph!" She rolled her eyes and groaned out a huff as the receiver clicked back into place.

Ellen looked up from behind the long, polished front counter, a postage stamp pinched between her thumb and forefinger. "The countdown begins."

"Five days." Nina held up her hand, her fingers splayed. "Alex's grandparents come Thursday, and the first guests check in Friday evening."

Ellen licked the stamp and stuck it on a tan-and-brown tri-folded brochure. "And the last of the reservation confirmations go out in tomorrow morning's mail."

As a light flutter filled Nina's stomach, she bit her lip to keep from giggling like a child at Christmas. "It looks like it's really going to happen, doesn't it?"

"Did you doubt it for one moment?" Clint pushed through the swinging doors that led into the dining room.

Immediately, Nina dropped her gaze to the open registration book on the counter. "Um, no, not really. It's just that—it's all gone by so quickly."

Everything but the last seven days, she thought, battling back the memory of the kiss they'd shared a week ago today. Since then, it seemed that time had dragged its feet. Maybe that was because she couldn't get past that event but kept thinking of it over and over again until she thought she'd scream. Or maybe the amount of energy she had spent avoiding Clint all week while trying to make it look as if she wasn't avoiding him had her so exhausted that everything felt slowed and sluggish. Or maybe—but it didn't matter why.

What mattered was that she remain detached, cordial yet cool, and completely disinterested in Clint Cooper as anything but a temporary business partner.

Clint moved around the counter so that he stood at her shoulder. "Nina?"

The deep masculine voice penetrated her anxiety.

"Hmm?" She gripped the corner of the book and tapped a pencil to the page, letting the eraser bounce over the half-dozen names.

"Barring any last minute emergencies, it looks like we're all set." He leaned, straight-armed, on the counter, one thumb hooked behind his rodeo championship belt buckle. "We could open the ranch tomorrow if we wanted to."

"Clint Cooper, have you lost your mind? We can't open tomorrow!" She jerked her head up and the pencil skidded down the paper, leaving pink rubble along a sharp crease. Okay, so she blew acting detached. But his remark warranted a response. "We're opening Friday."

"Of course we are." He tipped his hat back. "I know that. I just meant the place is good to go. No need to get all worked up."

"I'm not worked up." She tossed the pencil down and slammed the registration book closed with a whoosh that made her hair fan away from her face. The gust of air felt good on her hot cheeks. "Who's worked up? Not me."

"Yeah, right." He chuckled.

"Don't give me any of your attitude, bucko. I'm tired, and thanks to you and your cowboy cuisine, I've got so much salt and bacon grease in my system that I could deep fry your sorry hide with one well-placed glare."

"I feel it, I feel it." He held his hands up in mock surrender.

There went cordial yet cool.

Clint shifted his weight to his uninjured leg and sighed, something he rarely ever did. She cocked her head and narrowed her eyes, hoping to hide her concern with a scathing expression.

"Anyhow," he went on, "I've made a doctor's appointment for first thing tomorrow morning."

"A doc—" She stepped toward him, placing her hand on his arm. "Clint, are you okay?"

"Actually, I've never been better. Fact is, I'm hoping to get the doc's okay to get back to the circuit."

"The circuit? You mean the rodeo circuit?"

"None other."

"B-but, you can't."

He raised an eyebrow.

"That is, what about the ranch?"

"I won't be gone much at first. You know, take a few days off here and there to throw in with a local outfit, something within a day's driving distance. Just to get my hand in again." His eyes focused on the horizon through the lobby windows. "That way I'll be back in shape when I'm ready to hit it full-time in a few months."

"That'll be early fall, when the last of our booked guests will be leaving," she reminded him.

"I know."

"And there'll still be rodeos then?" She strummed her fingers on the countertop. "That late in the season?"

He chuckled. "There are rodeos year-round. I'll just have to go where they are, down south: New Mexico, Arizona, Texas."

"Sounds—" Far away, she thought, a strange ache that had no business being there building in her chest. "Exciting."

"Yeah, it's that all right, but…" His voice trailed off, his gaze remaining fixed in the distance. Sadness edged his features, and a sense of empty longing lingered in the air like the last word unspoken.

"Exciting but lonely?" she asked, just above a whisper.

"I don't get lonely." He bent his head. "At least I didn't."

But now? she wanted to ask. It was wrong to hope, but she did it all the same—that she and Alex might have touched Clint in some way that had him thinking twice about leaving them.

So much for being completely disinterested in Clint Cooper as anything but a temporary business partner.

"I haven't been lonely for a very long time, not since just after—"

She curled her fingers around his wrist to offer support and encouragement. He flinched at her touch, blinked at the place where her hand met his, then stepped back, withdrawing physically as well as emotionally.

"That's not important." He settled his hat down low over his eyes and drew up his shoulders. "I just wanted to let you know I'll be in town tomorrow morning for the appointment. Since we're all set, I didn't think the time away would hurt anything."

The time away, she thought, imagining the day when Clint rode off for good, would hurt everything. And yet she was helpless to change it. She still couldn't run the ranch, raise her son, and nurture a new relationship all at the same time. And even if she wanted to try—

She stole a glance at Clint from beneath her lowered lashes. Even if she wanted to try, this man wanted no part of it. It showed in the way he closed her out, in his drive to get back to the circuit, in his rigid stance as he nodded, turned, and strode out the front door into the bright sun.

"Gosh, I didn't realize he was going to try to ride again."

Nina started at the sound of Ellen's voice. Until now, she'd forgotten the girl stood within earshot of her whole conversation with Clint.

"Um, yeah," she muttered. "That's always been the plan. When I get the ranch on its feet and he gets himself on his, then he's history."

She sniffled and blinked away the tears that bathed her stinging eyes. With a great big phony smile plastered on her face, she tossed her head and shrugged for Ellen's benefit. "Nothing to be upset about, really. He'll be doing what he loves, and I'll have this whole new life and new business and everyone will be happy."

She walked with purpose toward the front door, then paused as she caught sight of Clint bending down to speak to Alex, who was digging a hole for no particular reason beside the freshly painted barn.

"Everyone will be happy, right?" she murmured again, unaware she'd spoken aloud until she heard Ellen's soft response from behind her.

"Yeah, right. Everyone's going to be just overjoyed, especially Alex."

~~~~~

"Going somewhere, Mr. Cooper?"

Clint shut one eye and pressed his lips together. Ellen. Just what he needed, the ranch busybody zeroing her highly trained gossip antennae on him. He took his horse's lead in one hand and brought the animal around so that both he and Ranger faced the young woman's bright expression. "If you must know, Ellen, I'm just taking a little ride."

"Ah, need to get away, do ya?" She put one foot on the splintered bottom rail of the corral fence. Behind her, Clint could see Alex, stamping dirt back into the hole he'd just dug by the barn. "Want some time to yourself to think?"

"Well, yeah, that's right." He patted Ranger's broad neck, his focus still on the young boy wiping his hand across his small nose.

"I don't blame you." She shook her head and her ponytail whipped from one ear to the other. "Don't blame you one bit. A man needs time alone."

Clint felt his brow crease in confusion. How could a young woman like this know what a man needed?

"My father always says so, at least."

"Oh, your father," he muttered, smiling at the sun on Alex's blond hair and his dirt-smudged face as the boy hitched up his pants and looked around for more mischief to get into.

Ellen folded her hands together. "My father always says, 'Comes a time a man just needs to get away, to leave his troubles behind so he can be alone with himself, his thoughts, and his God.'"

Clint let out a quiet snort and Ranger echoed it, as if he and the horse had drawn the same conclusion. "Your daddy sounds pretty smart."

"I think so." She smiled the way a daughter smiles when

she's bragging about her first hero. "He says if a man doesn't get away now and again, he runs the risk of getting so caught up in the work-a-day world and all his obligations and such that he stops being able to tell the difference between what he thinks he has to do and what's the right thing to do. I'm not sure I fully understand what he means by that."

"I do." He tore his gaze from the boy, hung his head, and ground his heel into the soft dirt.

"And that's why you're going off riding, then, right?"

"Yeah." He cleared his throat. "Yes, that's right."

"Want me to tell Mrs. Jackson any particular time that you'll be back?"

"I don't think Nina will be counting the hours till my return." He blew out a humorless chuckle.

"Well, you know how things are on a ranch, Mr. Cooper. You're always just one thunderstorm or a broken fence post away from another emergency."

"Ellen, weren't you there just a minute ago when I told Nina that I've gone over the whole place and everything is ready to roll?"

"Yes."

"And there's not a cloud in the sky, so I'm assuming Nina can live without me for the next hour or so." He tipped his hat to her and moved around to mount his horse.

"Gee, must not be too much on your mind, then, if it's only going to take an hour or so of riding to work it out." She made a face.

He paused, scowled for just a moment at her easy teasing, then broke into a laugh. "Actually, young lady, I could take from now till opening day alone and still not—"

"What a great idea!"

"What?"

"Taking from now until opening day off. You said so yourself;

131

there's nothing left to be done around the ranch, and you could really use a break."

"You're suggesting I just take off and—"

"Hey, Clint, you going riding?" Alex waved his arms wildly, then cupped his hands around either side of his mouth. "Can I go, too?"

Clint dragged his thumb along his bristled jaw line. Maybe getting away for a few days wasn't such a bad idea, after all.

"No, I can't just take off," he argued, more with himself than with Ellen. "I've got a doctor's appointment tomorrow morning, and then I want to be here on Thursday when Alex's grandparents show up. Where could I go in that length of time and still be reasonably available to Nina if she should need me?"

"Hmm." Ellen rested her knuckle against her chin. "That is a problem."

"Clint, can me 'n' Plinkey go with you? If you take us out on any of the riding trails you won't have to watch over me so much 'cause Plinkey practically knows the way all by himself." The small boy scooted between Ellen and Clint, his eyes bright with anticipation.

Ranger pawed the ground, restless to get moving. Clint tensed at the idea of spending any more time than he needed to with the boy. "You know, kid, maybe that's not such a—"

"It's perfect. Alex, you're a genius."

"I am?"

"He is?"

"Of course. Don't you know what you find if you go all the way up the riding trails?"

Alex stuffed his hands in his pockets and screwed his nose up. "Just those ol' mountain cabins."

"The—?" A slow smile crept over Clint's mouth. "Now, why didn't I think of that? I wonder if the trail is cleared enough for me to make it up there on horseback or if I'd need to take the road and use my truck?"

He said it only half aloud, but Ellen chimed in with a firm response. "Why don't you two ride up and check it out for yourselves? It's only about a forty-five minute ride."

Alex jumped and clapped his hands. "Can we, Clint? Can we?"

"Well, I don't know, kid." He kept from meeting the boy's hopeful gaze. A quick, dull tugging at his heart told him to seize this opportunity while he could. If he did go off to the mountain cabins and spend the next few days there, he'd use the time to purge his system of his feelings for Alex and Nina. That, as Ellen had put it, was the "right thing to do." This might be his last chance to spend time with the boy before he became the man he'd been before he came to Jackson's Butte Dude Ranch—solitary and self-contained.

"Maybe you and I can do something together, Alex," Ellen said, bending down to put her hand on the boy's shoulder. "Mr. Cooper wants some time alone to think."

"Think about what?"

About why he couldn't keep doing things like he was just about to do, Clint thought. He sighed, reached his hand out to Alex and said, "Never mind, son. Thanks to Ellen, I've got a plan to get plenty of time to think starting tomorrow after I get back from the doctor's."

She folded her arms and nodded, obviously pleased she had been of some help. "I'll let Mrs. Jackson know you're going riding and won't be home until late afternoon."

"Thanks, Ellen, for everything." He bent his head and narrowed his eyes at Alex. "Now, let's go saddle up that Doberman pinscher in a Shetland pony outfit and hit the trail."

Alex giggled and took Clint's hand. They both headed for the barn, with Ranger clomping along behind.

133

~ ~ ~ ~ ~

"I'll never be able to do this. Never." Nina tossed down her pencil and pressed her fisted hands against her aching eyes.

"Aw, it can't be all that bad, Mrs. J." Ellen tiptoed into the unpretentious office, a steaming mug of coffee in her hand. "Here. I thought I'd bring you this before I left for home. You look like you're hunkered in for a long night."

Nina drew in the rich aroma. "Thanks, Ellen. You're real sweet, but I don't think there's a night long enough for me to figure a way out of this."

"A way out?" Ellen leaned against the edge of the desk.

Nina shook her head. There was no way a young college girl could understand her financial—and emotional—difficulties. "I've just been going over the books, the long-term projections, the costs that have added up, and I just wish there were a way to earn more money faster."

"Speaking as a college student whose expenses are creeping up faster than a cheap pair of pantyhose, all I can say is, 'preach it, sister.'"

Nina laughed. For the first time this evening, she let herself relax and leaned back in her chair. The padding felt good against her tense muscles, and the laughter eased her battered heart.

"I thought things were going pretty well with the ranch." Ellen craned her neck and made a show of stealing a peek at the books and papers strewn over Nina's desk. "I didn't realize you were in that big of a money crunch."

"The ranch is fine, Ellen. The long-term outlook is much better than I'd originally expected, actually."

"Then why…?"

"Do I want to find a way to prime the money pump?"

Ellen nodded.

"Simple." At least that's how she intended to present it, as simply as possible.

Nina might be tired, but she wasn't punchy enough to let anything slip about her attraction to Clint. Imagine the rumors that information would fuel, and who knew what other nonsense. In the end none of that would matter. Clint was not a permanent fixture at Jackson's Butte Dude Ranch, and the sooner she found a way to send him on his way, the better it would be for all of them.

"I want to find a way between now and Thursday to increase my earning power so I can buy out Clint Cooper's share of the ranch." She reached for the cup of coffee and raised it to her lips. "I'll stay at this desk day and night if I have to until it's done."

"I knew things weren't right between you two," Ellen murmured. "But I really hoped you'd work it out."

Nina gulped down the hot, bitter brew quickly to keep from spraying it all over her paperwork. "Ellen, there is nothing to work out."

"I'm sorry you feel that way." Ellen's shoulders showed a definite slump. "Of course, the one I feel sorriest for is Alex."

Nina set the coffee cup down with a solid clunk. "Alex is not involved in this."

"You wouldn't say that if you saw the way that little boy looked when he went riding off with Clint this afternoon."

"I've seen Clint and Alex together, Ellen, believe me." And the sight always choked her up even as the mention of it did now. She gritted her teeth and forced the words out. "But this is between Clint and—"

"That's it!" Ellen smacked her hands together. "I can't believe I didn't think of this before."

Nina pulled her back up straight. "I have the feeling I'm going to regret asking this, but…you can't believe you didn't think of *what* before, Ellen?"

"Do you know where Alex and Clint rode today?"

"I'll take a wild guess—the riding trails?"

"Not just any riding trails, though. Clint wanted to see if he could ride all the way up." She stabbed one finger toward the ceiling as if the trail led to the roof.

"Up?" Nina imitated the gesture.

"Yes, up. Into the mountains and the mountain—"

"The mountain cabins!" Nina slapped a palm against her forehead. "Why didn't I think of that? I wanted to open those cabins from the very beginning, but Clint said—"

"So, you've already checked them out and know what it would take to get them outfitted?"

Nina propped her chin in her hand. "No, Clint talked me out of it. If only—"

"Why don't you do it now?"

Ellen's enthusiasm roused Nina's suspicions for a moment, but she quickly dismissed her uneasiness. What possible motive could Ellen have for promoting the mountain cabins? It would, after all, just mean more work for the staff. "Just what is it you're suggesting, Ellen?"

"Well, the ranch is ready to go, and Alex's grandparents aren't going to get here until Thursday.…"

"So, you think I should go up to the cabins every day and get some work done?" It wasn't a terrible idea.

"We-ell." Ellen wrung her hands. "Um, why go up every-day? Why not go up once and just stay?"

"Hmm." That was even less terrible than the first idea. Three days without the stress of seeing Clint everywhere she looked—and a chance to be productive as well. "That might work."

"Of course it will work. It has to work."

"What?"

"You know, so you can start earning extra money right away."

"Oh, uh-huh." Nina sat back and swirled the coffee inside the cup.

"And I'll take care of Alex for you."

"Oh, no, I couldn't ask that." She wanted Alex with her—and away from Clint.

"I don't mind really, and this isn't exactly the kind of thing you need an audience for." She folded her arms and laughed lightly.

"What isn't the kind of thing? Ellen, you're not making any sense."

"Oh, um, I guess it's late. I'm tired. What I meant was that if you're going to get any real work done, you don't want a little boy underfoot."

"Thanks for your concern, but I think he'll be fine." Nina patted the girl on the arm. "After all, it's only a few days, and I'm just going to test the cabins for living conditions. I'm sure Alex will be able to keep himself busy that long."

"Then you are going to go up there for sure?" The girl's eyes shone, and she grinned as if she'd just discovered calorie-free chocolate.

Nina bit her lip. She tapped her fingernail on the rim of the coffee cup.

Ellen raised her eyebrows and leaned forward to press the question.

Nina tried to weigh the pros and cons in her mind, but all she could consider was how easy this little getaway would make the next few days. Suddenly it was less about finding a new source of income and more about getting away from Clint. That was what she wanted most at this point. That was what she'd wanted ever since she had the first impossible stirrings of emotion for the man.

"Yes, Ellen, I am going up there."

"Yes!"

Nina scowled at the girl for a moment, then shrugged. "I can pack tonight and drive up as soon as Clint leaves to go into town to the doctor. And I don't want you to tell him where I've gone, even if he asks. Do you understand?"

"Oh, don't worry, Mrs. J. Mr. Cooper isn't going to find out about your trip from me. I can guarantee you that."

Chapter NINE

S o, this is it." Nina slammed the car door behind her and then dropped her weighty backpack onto the dusty ground.

She surveyed the setting in one fluid sweep of the eyes. The musty odor of forest and threatening rain filled her senses. The thick covering of leaves overhead rustled in the wind. Except for the sound of Alex getting out of the car, an eerie sense of quiet and solitude permeated the air.

Somehow when Ellen suggested this little excursion, Nina had not considered how cut off from everything and everyone she and Alex would be. Even with her pager and a cellular phone, they couldn't get back to the ranch and no one could get to them without a twenty-minute drive along a barely passable road. A cool breeze swirled around her. Nina shivered. Suddenly three days and nights alone in this remote area didn't seem like such a terrific idea.

If she were smart, she'd just call the whole thing off.

"Is that one of them, Mama?" Alex came around the car to stand beside Nina. In front of them, five paths wound away from the open area, each leading to a rustic cabin.

She followed the line of his pointing index finger. If she focused intensely enough, she thought she could just make out the wooden frame of a small cabin through the thick trees.

"I guess it is." She was tempted to smack her hands together, say "That's that," and trundle her child back to the relative civilization of the ranch. With great effort, she resisted the temptation.

"You guess? You mean you don't know?" He scratched his nose.

"No."

He cocked his head and folded his arms. "If Clint was here he'd know."

"If Clint *were* here, he'd know," she corrected.

"See, even you wish he was here," the boy muttered.

They'd gone around that mulberry bush time and again since she'd told Alex about the trip this morning. "Why isn't Clint coming?" "What will Clint do while we're gone?" "How are we going to get along without Clint?"

The questions still rang in her ears and reconfirmed for her the very reason she'd wanted to get away in the first place. Clint had already become too much a part of Alex's day-to-day life. It was time for a break. For that reason, she owed it to her son and to herself to at least investigate the accommodations.

"Well, even without the all-knowing Clint Cooper, Alex, it looks like we've stumbled on the famous mountain cabins."

"Stumbled on? You make it sound like an accident, Mama. Didn't you drive up and see them before?"

"Nope, honey, I've been too busy since we moved here." And before, she'd felt so much pressure from her in-laws about everything from raising Alex to where she should live, that she'd hardly been able to think. And when the opportunity came along to invest in the old Lazy H Dude Ranch and make it her own, she'd jumped at it.

This ranch and the surrounding land, it had seemed, was a bona fide answer to prayer. It gave her a home that provided the perfect atmosphere to raise Alex and a job that allowed her to keep her son close by. It was far enough from her in-laws that they couldn't drop in unannounced, but not so far that they couldn't come for a few days when they felt the urge. All these factors, plus the word of the previous owners and a pretty four-color brochure of the place, had sold her on the property.

Of course, that was far too much information for a child Alex's age to absorb.

Nina sighed and put her hands on her hips. "Honey, have you ever heard of buying a pig in a poke?"

"Mmm." He rubbed his hand in a circle over his tummy. "They're yummy."

Nina laughed and reached out to cup her son's chin in her hand. "You're thinking of a pig in a blanket—a hot dog wrapped in bread."

He exaggerated licking his lips. "I like 'em!"

"Well, I like those a whole lot better than a pig in a poke, too."

"What's a pig in a poke?"

"It's an expression that means buying something you haven't seen. You just take the word of the person who sells it to you that it's everything they say it is. See, it's like buying a pig in a poke, which is another word for sack."

He blinked up at her as though she'd started to speak pig Latin.

She tucked one strand of hair behind her ear, then tapped her fingernail against her chin, trying to decide how best to make her point. Finally, she folded her arms and said, "The thing is, honey, that's how I bought this ranch. Sight unseen. I trusted things would be, well, in better shape than they were."

"You mean it's a bad thing to trust people?"

"No." That was not the lesson she wanted to convey. She bent down to put herself at his eye level. "No, honey. We have to trust people, and more importantly, we put our trust in God. I prayed long and hard before I bought this place, and I did it because I felt it was the right thing to do for both of us."

He was trying to follow her. She saw it in his eyes and in the way his nose and mouth scrunched up in childish concentration as he listened.

"Anyway, the point is, I bought this ranch without knowing what I was getting. That's why we're here today, to see what we've got in these mountain cabins. I want you to understand that if they're in really bad shape, we can't stay the night like we'd planned."

He thrust his lower lip out, dug the toe of his shoe into the dirt, and narrowed one eye. "You promised."

The soft rumbling of thunder underscored his discontent with her.

Nina glanced up through the lacy canopy of trees at the gray sky overhead and sighed.

"If Clint was here, I bet he'd—"

"Well, Clint is not here. I am, and I say—"

"You said you trusted in God."

That she had. She pressed her lips together.

"Well, don't you still?"

"Yes, of course I do, honey." She stretched up on tiptoe to peer down the largest of the five paths at the outline of the crude cabin through the woods. "But this place is so isolated and rugged; not what we're used to at all."

"So we should only trust God when things are the way we're used to?" He bounced from one foot to the other as he spoke.

"No, we should trust God all the time; in all things, and in all circumstances."

"But not now?"

142

Nina knew when she was licked. She smoothed back a lock of Alex's fine blond hair and shifted her feet in the dust of last year's fallen leaves. "Well, they're supposed to be rustic. I guess if we find one with four walls and a roof, we can stay. We did bring plenty of camping supplies, after all, and plenty of cleaning supplies to square things away. But if I decide there isn't a safe cabin to stay in, we're coming home with no complaints. Deal?"

"Deal." He stuck out his hand like a man.

She shook his hand, then gave him a quick kiss on the cheek to seal their bargain.

"Aw, Mama." He scrubbed at the spot on his cheek that her lips had brushed. "I'm getting too big for that stuff."

"You're never too big for a kiss, young man."

"When you and Clint shake hands you never kiss him," he pointed out.

"Yes, well, that's different." An angry boom of thunder sounded in the distance. Nina plucked up her overstuffed backpack and slung it over one shoulder. "And speaking of Clint, didn't you and he look into any of the cabins when you rode up here yesterday?"

"He did. We found a back road that circled all the cabins, and a stream. So he walked along the road to see the cabins while I watered the horses." He puffed up his chest with pride. "Then I looked for wild animal tracks."

"Did you find any?" She clutched at the strap of her backpack, a flutter of anxiety rising in her belly.

"Nope."

She blew out a breath like an almost silent whistle. "Good, then let's go find our home away from home for the next few nights. We've got five cabins to choose from; at least one of them has to be fit to inhabit."

~ ~ ~ ~ ~

Five cabins, and only one of them even remotely resembled the picture of rustic coziness in the glossy brochure Nina had tacked to the bulletin board in her office. Clint parked his truck behind a row of bushy pines that hid from his view the one cabin that wasn't an absolute disaster.

What was he doing here? He gripped the steering wheel and glowered up at the threatening sky. It didn't take a genius to realize that if anything more than a gentle rain fell today, he'd be flat out stranded. The roads were nothing but barren tracks of back-hoed dirt just waiting for a good soaking to make them slippery slopes of tire-grabbing mud. The riding paths had not been cleared, so rain would make them treacherous even to a man with two good legs. For him...

He rubbed his thigh and flexed his calf muscle, but that did not ease the ever-present aching left over from his long ride yesterday. He thought of the doctor's prognosis for a full recovery—one that would allow him to return to the rodeo circuit—and grunted in disgust. He wasn't going back to anything. The news hadn't surprised him. At thirty-three, his career was near its close anyway. But lately, with the uncomfortable state of his growing feelings for Nina, he had been hoping for anything to justify his leaving the ranch.

He relaxed his leg, putting his foot flat on the floorboard, and his knee popped in protest. Thunder rattled the truck windows.

A man with more sense would turn around and hightail it out of here, he supposed. But then a man with more sense wouldn't have taken his life's savings and invested them in a dude ranch that wouldn't see profits until who knew when. A man with more sense would never have gotten himself tangled up with a woman who didn't know when to say quit, who didn't care how great the odds were against her success. A woman who didn't realize that with a smile she could make this battered old cowboy's day and with a tear she could break his heart.

He took a deep breath and opened the truck door. He'd come up here to forget about Nina—to rein in the feelings she stirred up, not to get all mushy over her.

The truck dipped as he slid out. A deep bass roll of thunder coincided with his slamming the door. Another accompanied his dropping the tailgate. He scooped up the box of supplies he'd gathered from the ranch and from town and headed for the cabin.

"Well, I'll be," Clint muttered, shouldering open the cabin's back door. He pocketed the master key he'd taken from the set of four hanging in the ranch office, then settled the heavy box on the floor.

The window he'd peered through yesterday must have distorted the view, he decided. This place wasn't nearly as bad as he'd expected. The floor looked clean, the furniture in good shape. He ran one fingertip along the surface of the kitchen table. The place hadn't even collected much dust standing empty all winter.

He scratched his head just under his cowboy hat, then tugged the collar of his denim jacket up and headed back out to the truck to get his sleeping bag and the camping gear he might not need after all.

He rounded the stand of pines that lined the cabin along the east side. A cool breeze assaulted him and lightning flickered in the distance. The storm would hit with full force within the hour, he figured. By then, if he really moved his beat-up excuse for a hind end, he could have his bedding laid out, the lantern lit and—his gaze fell on a battered ax angled up from a sturdy log.

A fire. The perfect touch. Since it was almost summer, he hadn't thought about having a fire. He'd brought food in an ice chest and anticipated living on a simple diet of sandwiches, cheese, and fruit. He hadn't planned on cooking. But now the notion of chopping his own wood for a fire touched something basic within him.

The exercise, he decided, was just the thing to drive away the sluggishness of his mood. He picked through the pile of weathered logs and found a nice piece to stand on end on the chopping block. He seized the ax handle and brought the blade down with a smooth, hard blow.

It wasn't long before he had a hefty armload of wood and kindling, enough for a couple nights' worth of fires. His injured leg quivered under the weight of the load, but he made his way determinedly to the cabin. Just outside the back door, the pain had grown to a throb. He took another step, then stumbled forward, falling onto one knee.

He shouldn't have tried to do so much. Yesterday's long ride had really been too much too soon, and this certainly hadn't helped. He let the wood roll from his arms and groaned softly.

A fat raindrop plopped in the loose dirt. He reached out and used the doorknob to pull himself to his feet. The door swung in slightly before he made it completely to his feet. Another raindrop came down and then another. He gritted his teeth and pivoted, determined to get his bedding in and then to bring in the wood before it became soaked. After that, he could sit and relax for three whole days. There would be nothing to distract him.

"Alex, close that door!" Nina twisted her neck to peer from her bedroom door through the cabin's great room and into the open kitchen, where the breeze she felt was fluttering the curtains above the sink. "Alex?"

No response.

"What is that boy up to now?" she muttered as she flung the blanket over her bed then headed out of her room. "There is no way he could have made up his bed already and gone out to play." She raised her voice. "Alex?"

A raindrop splattered against the wooden roof, followed quickly by several more.

"If that child has gone out to play in this weather…"

She marched across the room to the partially opened back door and yanked it wide, drawing a deep breath to call out her son's name.

"What do you want, Mama?" a small voice asked from behind.

Nina jumped. She twisted her head to find her son standing in the doorway to his own bedroom. She sighed. "I want you to learn to close a door. Is that asking too much?"

"Huh?"

She rolled her eyes at his casual attitude toward common sense and started to close the door. A cluster of cool raindrops bombarded her shoes and arm, drawing her attention. She glanced outside.

"Oh, look at this. Here's a pile of firewood left over from last season. What do you say we bring it in so it doesn't get wet?"

"Okay!" came Alex's eager reply. "If Clint was here, he could start a fire!"

"I don't need Clint Cooper starting anything for me." Nina's hand flew to cover her lips. Had she actually said that? Good thing the man wasn't here; she could just imagine the teasing he'd give her! She pictured his intense eyes and rakish grin and felt a flush creep up her neck. Even when he wasn't here, he started things for her—things she'd come all this way to escape.

Nina stepped outside the cabin, almost expecting the raindrops that struck her to sizzle with the heat of her blush. She gathered up as much wood as she could hold and carried it inside, kicking the door shut behind her. The logs fell with a thump into a corner next to a rocker near the fireplace just as another smattering of rain hit the roof.

"Oh, you know what, Alex? I left the matches in the car. I'd better run get them before the rain really starts coming down."

"Can I come with you, Mama? I forgot my pillow in the backseat."

"Okay, but come quick." She opened the front door and motioned for him to hurry. "We'll have to make a run for it."

"Cooper, you are losing it." Clint hitched up the sleeping bag under his arm and poked the toe of his cowboy boot at the pathetic little pile of wood that had literally brought him to his knees. "I could have sworn I chopped more wood than that. I really am out of shape—and talking to myself to boot."

The door creaked as he went inside, planning to toss his sleeping bag onto a bed and then go back for the pitiful bundle of logs and kindling.

The door opened into a great room, bracketed by a stone fireplace on one side and the eating/kitchen area on the other. A wobbling table, four mismatched chairs, a free-standing cupboard, and a stainless steel sink filled the space to his left. A wood-framed couch, mustard yellow with dark brown eagles clutching green olive branches in their talons, was set square in the middle of the room. Next to it was a recliner that had probably once been olive green beneath all the duct tape holding it together. A big rocker peeked out from the shadowy corner near the fireplace. Tying it all together, a piece of orange-and-red shag carpeting was haphazardly tossed over the floorboards.

"And Nina thought she'd be able to charge good money to

rent these places out," he muttered, shaking his head. He headed for the closest bedroom to stow his things.

"Uh-uh. This will have to go." He nudged his sleeping bag under the spindly twin bed, then bent to pull off the crumpled sheets left on since last season. His fist wadded the red, blue, and yellow cowboys into a ball as he offered his best attempt at a John Wayne accent. "Wa-ahl, come on pilgrims, this bed ain't big enough for the both of us. If I didn't know better, I'd say you bunch of bacteria-ridden buckaroos were the handiwork of a certain greenhorn boss lady."

What was he doing? He let the sheets fall into a heap at the foot of the bed.

"You're not just talking to yourself, Cooper. You're doing bad impressions to entertain the linen," he grumbled. "Keep this up, and by Thursday you'll be giving pet names to the pots and pans and acting out puppet plays with your dirty socks!"

Outside, the thunder roared and the rain began to fall at a steady beat.

"Much as I'd like to stay here and argue with myself," he said under his breath as he headed for the back door, "if I want a fire tonight, I've got a date with an ax."

"Mama, can I lay out the wood for the fire?" Alex blew into the cabin like a tornado, swinging the front door open with such energy that the backdraft made the back door slam shut.

"Hmm. I thought I shut that back door." Nina followed more slowly as Alex ran across the cabin, heading straight for the pile of wood hidden by the rocker. "You can stack the wood in the fireplace, but do not try to light it. You got that, young man? Alex?"

His lower lip poked out in a pout. "Got it."

She hugged the pillow they'd retrieved from the car to her

chest and watched her son. This was exactly what she needed: no ranch pressure, no visit from the in-laws looming, no Clint Cooper to tell her she was doing everything wrong, wrong, wrong.

The thought of the man she'd come here to avoid sent a shiver down her spine. His presence seemed suddenly real to her, and very near. She jerked her head up, half expecting to find his intense gaze fixed on her. But the cabin was just as she'd left it.

What foolishness. Clint was back at the ranch, probably quite content to have found her and Alex gone for the next few days. Drawing in a deep breath of cabin air and freshly washed linen, she moved to Alex's room to put his pillow away before she helped him get the fire started. She stopped abruptly in the bedroom doorway.

"Alex! Didn't I tell you to make your bed up?"

"Yes, ma'am."

She stared at the bedraggled sheets tumbling over the foot of the bed. "Then I suggest you get yourself in here and do it—now!"

"But Mama—"

"Don't you 'but Mama' me, young man. March yourself in here and do as I've asked."

"But—"

"March!"

Clint's boot slid in the already muddy ground outside the cabin. Biting down on the urge to let loose his frustration, he clutched the freshly split logs against his damp shirt. The cloudburst that had rushed him inside before he could get more wood chopped, pounded down on the cabin roof with unleashed fury. Planning to shut the door after he unloaded the wood, he took several long strides across the floor.

"Oh, great," he ground out between clenched teeth. "I spent all that time chopping wood and there was already some left in the fireplace."

He set his wood aside, straightened, and whisked his hat off, dripping rainwater on his already damp jeans. The back of his shirt was soaked, his jeans splattered with mud. A nice hot fire would really hit the spot right now. He picked up a box of matches from the hearth.

"Tuck that corner in, Alex." Nina pointed to the end of the bed. "Then we'll smooth this down and be all done."

"Again."

Nina sighed. "Don't start with me, Alex. All I want right now is to get a nice fire going, get some lunch, and then relax."

Alex plopped his pillow in place and gave it a punch.

Nina smiled, nodded her approval of a job well done, and stood aside while Alex scampered ahead of her.

"You know, Mama, I'll bet we'd have a real good fire already if Clint was here to make it."

"Alex, for the millionth time, the last person I would want up here in this isolated cabin with us is—"

Her feet came to an abrupt halt. Her heartbeat did the same when she saw the figure of a man, his head stuck in the fireplace while his hands worked at the chimney flue.

Nina swallowed. She'd know those broad shoulders and that long line of a back anywhere.

"Clint Cooper, what on earth are you doing here?"

151

Chapter

TEN

"O h, Clint, look out for the—"

Clang!

"—Flue handle."

The sudden metallic ringing in Clint's ears competed with the sharp eye-popping pain in the back of his head.

"Nina?" He staggered backward a step, cupped his hand to the back of his head, and searched for her over his shoulder. "What are you doing here?"

"Me?" She stabbed her finger into her chest. "What about you?"

He didn't owe her an explanation. Wasn't he half owner of this property? Wasn't he his own man, free to come and go as he pleased? Wasn't he just about to ask the very same question of her? He rubbed his fingers through his hair. "I'm here to get away for a few days."

"*I'm* here to get away for a few days."

"Didn't we go through this whole echo routine once before?" He shut his eyes and gingerly probed the rising lump at the back of his head.

Alex giggled.

Clint opened one eye to give the child a mock menacing look. "And I suppose you're here to get away for a few days as well?"

Alex nodded, his head bobbing forward and back as if his neck were a spring.

Clint fought back a smile. "I'd ask what it is you two think you have to get away from, but I'm not sure I'd like the answer. You didn't bring that vampire pony along, did you?"

Alex giggled again. "Plinkey's not a vampire."

"Well, you wouldn't know it to see all the teeth marks he's left on me," Clint grumbled good-naturedly.

The boy set his hands on his hips. "Vampires bite people on the neck, don't you know that? Plinkey always bites you—"

Clint held his hand up. "I'm reminded of where that set of chompers with a horse attached bites me every time I take a seat, kiddo."

Alex giggled again.

How Clint enjoyed that sound, even if it was offered at his own expense. In truth, the boy's ornery Shetland had never left so much as a red spot through the tough denim of his jeans. That fact, and the pony's fierce protectiveness of Alex, which Clint could fully appreciate, allowed him to keep his good humor about the nasty tempered animal.

He slid his hand down past the bump on his head to rest at the base of his neck. The room fell silent except for the rain that raged outside, sometimes coming down in sheets so heavy that it drowned out the sound of the intermittent thunder.

"Alex, honey, go close the back door." Nina put her hand to the boy's shoulder and gave him a nudge in the right direction. "Then why don't you get yourself a juice box and cookie and sit at the table there for a snack."

The boy did as he was told. The closed door helped dull the sound of the rain as well as cut off the draft. It did nothing to

154

warm the chilly tension between them.

"Anyway," Clint finally said, clapping his hands together, "looks like we had the same idea at the same time."

"I'm not so sure about that." Nina moved behind the massive couch and leaned her forearms on its back. "In fact, I really doubt if we had the same idea at all, Clint."

"What do you mean?" Clint settled slowly onto the cold stone hearth.

"The truth is, Clint, I didn't just come up here to relax. It's more of a working getaway for me."

"Working? What could you possibly be working on up here in this not-fit-for-fair-market-value cabin?"

She lowered her chin and gave him a steady, humorless look.

A flash of lightning filled the window over her shoulder.

"Oh, no. No, no. You can't seriously be thinking—" He rested an elbow on his thigh, shook his head, and laughed. "Not these cabins, Nina. Have you checked them out? This is the only one with furniture. One of the other cabins has a leaky roof, and two others look like they might have serious structural problems."

"Don't you think you're overstating things a bit?"

"No. We barely got the ranch cabins in rental condition in time. What do you hope to accomplish with these dilapidated shells? Open a roach motel?"

"I swept this place from top to bottom, Clint Cooper, and did not find a single roach."

"Oh, excuse me. A rodent roadside inn, then?"

"If you're trying to be funny—"

"I'm trying to be realistic, Nina." He stretched out his aching leg before him. "Look at this place. You can't possibly think to charge someone money to stay here."

"Why not? I think it's—"

155

"Tacky?"

She narrowed her eyes. "Quaint."

He raised his eyebrows to question that description.

"I think it's got a nice Early American feel to it," she said.

He glanced around the room. "Yeah, it does kind of look like something built in the 1700s."

"Ha-ha."

"Hearkens back to a time when men were men and women were women." He stole a peek at her, her shoulders drawn up all proper and prissy and her lips pursed. Maybe if he could get her to crack a smile, she'd see the foolishness of her idea—and then go home and leave him in peace. "Back in the days when great herds of savage couches the size of mastodons roamed these parts, just waiting to be tamed into submission."

One corner of her mouth twitched.

"And come evening, Pa would sit himself down in his over-stuffed, pillow-backed, gen-yoo-ine crushed velvet recliner."

He could see the bulge in her cheek as she poked her tongue there to keep from smiling.

"And recount the harrowing tale of the night he wuz attacked by a ferocious, man-eating, rare, red-and-orange shaggy-backed beast—which he killed barr-handed and what's hide lays here on the floor to this very day." He pointed to the ratty rug at his feet.

And she laughed. Not an all-out, hardy-har laugh, but a laugh, just the same.

"Okay, so it's ugly. That doesn't mean it's unrentable."

"Are you honestly telling me that you would stay here under any other circumstances?"

"Yes, I would."

He leaned forward. "And pay money to do it?"

She cocked her head, her hair moving gently around her big blue eyes. "What about you?"

"What about me what?"

"Are you saying that you wouldn't want to stay here?"

"Are you kidding? One look at this place and I'd hit the road so fast I would leave tread marks."

"Good."

"Good?" He'd meant to goad her into rethinking her plans. Now what was she up to? "What do you mean, good?"

"I mean good—since you don't want to stay here and I do, that just about solves the whole issue, doesn't it?"

"What issue?"

"The issue of who stays and who goes." She stood. "I stay and you—" She waved her hand in the direction of the door.

"Wait a minute. I'm not going anywhere."

"Well, we can't stay here together, now can we? How would that look?"

Never mind how it would look. How would it feel? Clint's gaze moved from Nina to Alex, then back to Nina. It would feel lousy. He'd come up here to purge his system of all thoughts of these two, not to deepen the bonds.

"Granted we both can't stay here, but where is it written that I have to be the one to leave?"

"Because it's my—"

"I wouldn't go there if I were you—partner."

She batted her thick lashes. "Um, well, um—I got here first. And I spent most of the morning cleaning the place up. What did you do?"

"Chopped all the firewood, for starters."

Her gaze fell to the wood in the grate, then moved to the pile on the floor behind the rocker, finally resting on the smaller stack beside the door.

"So, how are we going to decide who stays and who goes?" She crossed her arms.

A quick burst of lightning illuminated the cabin to its

rafters, followed an instant later by a roll of thunder overhead.

"Unfortunately, that may have been decided for us." Clint turned to look at the rain pelting the window. "I really don't think it's safe to take on these roads in these conditions."

"Oh, that's just—" She spun to face the kitchen area, where Alex was watching them with curious eyes. "Alex, are you done with your snack yet?"

"Almost," came the answer, muffled by his mouthful of cookie.

"Well, grab up what you've got left and bring it with you." Nina turned her determined gaze to Clint. "We're leaving."

"Oh, no, you don't." He leaped up and cut her off as she headed for the front door.

"One of us has to go and if it's not going to be you, then it's going to be me. End of discussion."

"End of discussion because there is no discussion." He put his hand on her arm to try to make her listen. "Didn't you hear what I said? It's not safe to travel these roads in this weather."

"C'mon, Alex." She kept her eyes on Clint's but jerked her hand away and stepped toward the door.

"Fine." He took a few long strides across the room, picked up his hat, and crammed it on.

She opened the door but stopped Alex from going through as she frowned at Clint. "And just what do you think you're doing?"

The pressure of his hat made Clint remember the painful knot on the back of his head. He winced but kept his voice level as he explained, "I'm going to follow you."

"Follow me? Why?"

"Because no way am I letting you take off in this weather, while I sit here all tucked in a cabin, hoping you make it back to the ranch all right."

"Well, if you're going to leave, then I don't have to go." She gave the door a shove and it went swinging shut.

"If you're not going to go, then I don't have to follow you." He removed his hat with an inward sigh of relief.

"So, in other words, either we both go or we both stay?"

"Looks like it." He leaned forward to place his hat on the back of one of the kitchen chairs.

"Fine. Then I'm going." She yanked the front door open again and ushered Alex out into the downpour, slamming the door behind her.

"Fine. Then I'm following." He plunked his hat on, pulled open the back door, and stepped out into what felt like a waterfall plummeting from the roof. So much for his time away from Nina, his time to reflect and relax. His solitary mountain cabin retreat had just turned into a family affair.

Under his breath he counted to three, then turned around and walked through the cabin door once again.

Nina flung open the front door and slogged across the threshold. She stopped, making Alex bump into her from behind, when she saw Clint glowering at her from the frame of the open back door.

"All right. Here's how it's gonna work." She slashed her hand through the air with finality. "You stay in one room, Alex and I in the other. We share our food and our responsibilities as much as is reasonable. And the minute—the absolute minute it is dry enough for one of us to leave, we draw straws and the loser is o-u-t, out. Deal?"

"Deal."

"Mama?" Alex tugged at the dripping hem of her shirt. "Aren't you forgetting something?"

She stepped fully inside the room and let the door fall shut. "What?"

"You know, when you make a deal with someone?"

"Oh yeah." She dropped the soggy bundle in her arms, stepped over the heap, and marched across the room.

Clint shut the back door and peeled off his hat as he wiped his muddy boots on the threadbare welcome mat.

"This makes it official," she said, swinging out her open hand to him.

"What?" He eyed the gesture as though it might be a trick.

Nina coughed to cover her chuckle at the image of her seizing Clint by the hand, bending his arm behind his back, and throwing him out the door. "Our arrangement, silly. We made a deal, didn't we?"

"Oh, sure." He fit his hand to hers. The touch, warm despite its moisture, made Nina catch her breath. He lowered his eyelids and his voice and gave her a smile that she could have poured over pancakes. "Sure. It's a deal."

She said nothing.

He said nothing.

"Mama?"

Nina nearly jumped from her skin and jerked her hand away from Clint's. "What?"

"You forgot the rest of it."

"The rest?" She blinked and ran her fingertips across her lower lip. "What rest?"

"Well, when you made a deal with me, you gave me a kiss on the cheek."

She froze. Her gaze flicked upward to meet Clint's.

He smiled again, rainwater sparkling in his hair, his shirt clinging to his shoulders and strong arms.

It would be so easy, she realized, to move one step closer and plant a chaste kiss on his cheek. But not so easy, she knew, to step away again.

"Aren't you going to kiss Clint?" Alex asked.

"I only did that because you're my son, Alex. That's not how friends do things."

"I don't know. It sounds like a pretty friendly way to come to terms to me," Clint murmured. "Right neighborly, you might say."

"We're not neighbors. We're business partners, and don't you forget that, Clint Cooper." She said his name, but she could just as well have said her own. *Don't you forget, Nina Jackson, that this man is here on business, transient business. He is not the kind of man you give a kiss to, because he is not the kind of man who can accept your love.*

She pivoted and threw back her head. A slippery strand of hair swung out to slap against her cheek. She ignored it and walked with dampened dignity to her bedroom.

The day dragged by in strained quiet. Alex and Clint played a board game Nina had brought along, then worked on a puzzle. After staring out the window for a while at the rain, Alex finally occupied himself drawing pictures. After dinner, they gathered around the fire. Nina nestled into the beat-up chair, her Bible in her lap.

The storm had died down to a gentle, steady drumming of rain on the roof. Clint eyed the rafters from his spot on the sagging sofa, expecting to feel a drip at any moment.

Alex scooted across the room and threw himself onto the sofa next to Clint, making the sad piece of furniture shudder. "Read us one with rain in it, Mama."

"Rain, huh? Let me look that up in the concordance." The delicate pages of the Bible fluttered as Nina thumbed to the back.

Clint watched her in the firelight, aware of Alex squirming next to him. If he wasn't careful, he might let himself enjoy this

161

precious moment out of time. He didn't want to enjoy it, didn't want to let this oasis of home and hearth get beneath the thick skin he'd developed since losing Jamie and Mark. He pushed his shoulders back against the lumpy cushion and stared into the fire.

"Hmm, there's one that mentions spring rain specifically. Let's read that one." Nina flipped through the thick book.

Alex bounced on the couch.

Clint folded his arms over his chest.

"It's Hosea 6," she said, her face the picture of concentration as she read ahead. "Okay, I'm going to read verses 1 through 3. Ready?"

"Ready," Alex reported.

Clint harrumphed.

"'Come, let us return to the LORD.'"

The words seemed chosen just for him. Clint pushed the heel of his boot along the rough shag of the carpet.

"'He has torn us to pieces...'"

Yes, Clint thought, the verse was for him.

"'But he will heal us; he has injured us but he will bind up our wounds.'"

Clint's eyes shifted to take in the scene of tranquillity about him. He thought of his own wounds and how much healing he'd felt these last few weeks.

"'After two days he will revive us; on the third day he will restore us, that we may live in his presence.'"

Just for me. Clint's crossed arms fell open.

"'Let us acknowledge the LORD; let us press on to acknowledge him.'"

He leaned forward.

"'As surely as the sun rises, he will appear; he will come to us like the winter rains, like the spring rains that water the earth.'" She pressed the book closed.

Clint shook his head, as if to dislodge the odd feeling that the verse, written so long ago, had spoken to him, to his personal situation.

"Okay, Alex, what do you think that meant?" Nina tilted her head, her hair falling sleek and shiny against her rosy cheek, her eyes glowing in the firelight.

The sight struck Clint's already shaken spirit like a physical blow. He swept his hand back over his head and staggered to his feet, then looked down to Alex and Nina. "I'm sorry, I think I should go on to bed now."

"Why, Clint?" Concern shone in the depths of Nina's eyes. "Is something wrong?"

"I—I just don't belong here, that's all."

"But I thought you liked the Bible, Clint." Alex wriggled around to stare up at Clint. "You go to our church and all."

"I go to your church, but we don't go there together. There's a reason for that and a reason why I don't have any business participating in your family Bible study."

"But why?" Alex's nose crinkled.

Because we are not now nor will we ever be a family, Clint wanted to shout.

"Mr. Cooper is my business partner, Alex, as well as our foreman, and hopefully our friend." Nina looked to Clint for reassurance.

He gave a brisk nod.

"He's not part of our family, and if this kind of family time makes him uncomfortable, then we should respect that. Now, tell him good night."

Clint saw her annoyance in her eyes and in her stiff posture. But he didn't care, he told himself. He was long past caring about those things—about anything.

"Good night," he mumbled. Turning his back on the woman and child and on the verses that haunted him, he retreated into his bedroom and into the safety of his own emotionless world.

The brilliant morning sun streaked over the foot of Nina's bed. As she stared at the patterns the light made on the wall, yesterday's events seemed precious, and she regretted that she hadn't appreciated them as they happened. But Clint had been right to break up the evening. It was dangerous to start feeling as if they were a family.

She threw back the bedcovers and stood, aware that Alex had gotten up from his sleeping bag on the floor. Let him spend a few more minutes with Clint, she decided, because as soon as she got dressed, she was going to go out there and bust up their togetherness with the toss of a coin.

With determination, she swung open the door and stepped into the great room. "Heads or—" She glanced around the quiet room, the shiny quarter like ice as she clutched it tight in her palm. "Alex? Clint?"

Birds chirped. The curtain from the open kitchen window flapped up with a sudden breeze, then fell back like a deflated balloon.

Nina turned in a full circle. The other bedroom door stood open, the room empty, as was the bathroom. She was alone.

"Hmm." She sighed. "I don't suppose they went back to the ranch together and left me here alone."

Alex erupted through the back door, a meager fish dangling from a hook raised high in his hand. "Mama! Look! I caught a fish!"

Nina stuck her tongue out. "Eeuuw. I see."

"Clint said you'd act like a girl when you saw it," he informed her as he started to hoist the fish onto the kitchen table.

"Whoa. Not there, honey." She jabbed the quarter into her

pocket, then rushed forward to save the pictures Alex had drawn the day before from a fishy fate.

"Not too shabby, eh?" Clint strode into the room with a fishing line in his fist. He lowered his day's catch into the sink. "Put 'em in here, pal."

Alex trotted over. His pungent prize flopped into the sink with a *thwump*.

"Looks like you two have been busy." Nina leaned her hip against the wall, her arms folded over Alex's artwork.

"Clint showed me how to do everything. Next time we come up here, I'm going to catch the food all by myself."

"Next time?" Nina raised an eyebrow. They hadn't even gotten through this time.

"Yeah, you know, when we come here for family vacations," Alex said with a brilliant smile. "Clint says it's perfect for that."

"Clint says?" She eyed the man in question.

"Well, that *is* what these cabins are for, Nina. Family vacations. I may have mentioned that to Alex; you know how it is when a couple guys get to yammering and fishing."

"It was great, Mama. Clint says the best time to go is first thing in the morning." Alex's eyes shone. She didn't think she'd ever seen him looking this happy.

The sight sent her maternal red flag up. She'd planned this trip to size up the cabins and to interrupt the bonding process between Clint and Alex. The cabins, she'd realized even before Clint told her, could not be readied for rental this season. So that much of her mission was over. She still had time to accomplish the second phase of her goal, however—to put some space between Alex and the man he believed he'd prayed into their lives to become his father.

Alex threw his chest out and poked his thumbs into his belt loops. "Clint says you gotta get up pretty early if you want to be a real fisherman."

Nina stole a sidelong glance at Clint and found his stance similar but a bit more relaxed than Alex's, his thumbs tucked behind his championship belt buckle.

"Clint says that's when the fish are really biting."

"Oh, he does, does he?" The papers crackled as she hugged them closer.

Alex rubbed his hand against his jeans, wiping the stream slime off his palm, and nodded with enthusiasm. "Fresh caught fish make the best breakfast when you're roughing it; that's what Clint says."

"And does Clint also say who's going to clean the fish?"

Alex giggled. "Fish aren't dirty, Mama; they live in water!"

"Um, when your mama says clean the fish, she means cut them up to be cooked." Clint cleared his throat and ducked his head. "I'll do that, Nina, and cook them, too."

"And eat them as well," she said.

"What? You mean you don't like fish?" His eyebrows drew together.

"I have nothing against fish."

"Just not for breakfast?"

"Alex, honey, why don't you go into the bathroom and scrub up real good. Wash your hands and face and—" She narrowed her eyes at him and made a show of sniffing him up and down. "In fact, why don't you just peel out of those clothes and take a quick shower?"

Alex laughed at the face she made. "Okay, Mama."

She held her breath as he scurried off, waiting until the bathroom door had fallen shut with a firm clunk before she nailed Clint with a steely glare. "Just what did you think you were doing, going off with him this morning without asking me?"

He stroked his chin, his eyes hooded in a sly, teasing expression. "Well, I checked in on you this morning when I got the boy up and thought about waking you. But you just looked so peaceful and angelic, I didn't have the heart to."

"Peaceful? Angelic?" She slapped the papers down on the table. "Me?"

"Yeah, surprised me, too. That's why I didn't disturb you. Figured something as rare as that—"

"Spare me the comedy." She rolled her eyes. Standing tall, she wiggled her fingers into her jeans pocket to retrieve the quarter. Pinched between her thumb and forefinger, the coin winked in the morning light. "We have serious business to tend to."

His big shoulders slumped forward a bit. "I know."

"If you knew, then why did you take Alex off fishing? Didn't you realize that this little stunt would only make it harder for him when…if—"

"When," he affirmed.

She nodded. "When one of us has to go?"

His gaze dropped, and he shifted, running one hand through his sun-streaked brown hair.

The sound of rumbling water in the pipes told Nina that time was running out. "Look, Clint, we don't have a lot of time. I'd like to have this mess settled before Alex comes back out here."

"Sure. But can we go over to the couch and settle it?" He swept his hand out as an invitation for her to lead the way. "All the riding two days ago, the rain yesterday, and sitting on a cold, damp rock before dawn this morning has this leg of mine in knots."

"Your leg?" She blinked.

In the chaos of preparing for the getaway and the hubbub of finding shelter from the storm, she'd forgotten all about Clint's leg and his doctor's appointment. She sank into a hollow spot in the rickety sofa, then crossed her legs, trying to look as if she'd meant to nearly fall through the stained cushions. "So your leg is still bothering you? What did the doctor say?"

"I'm fine, Nina." He shifted in the patched recliner.

"You don't act fine."

He shifted again, his hand gripping the arm until his knuckles went white.

"Clint?"

"I'm fine." He ground out the deliberate words between his clenched teeth.

Nina propped her foot up against the couch frame to keep from slipping completely through to the floor. "Is that what the doctor said?"

He winced and directed his gaze toward the window. "What do doctors know?"

"Oh, absolutely. You're right." She laid Alex's drawings aside and put both feet on the floor. "All those years of schooling, internship, residency. Just a big waste of time. And all those diplomas and certificates on their walls—just an excuse to overcharge you for their fancy guesswork."

"Something like that."

"Oh, Clint." She shook her head.

"What?"

"I'm just glad Alex isn't in here to hear this."

"Hear what?" He adjusted his body once again.

"You—lying."

He scowled. "I'm not lying."

"Okay, then tap dancing around the truth."

"Nina, trust me, I have never tap-danced around anything in my entire life."

She leaned forward, her elbows on her knees. "And it's my guess, from the way you're acting with that leg, that you never will."

"Yeah, well, that's tap dancing's big loss," he grumbled.

"And what about the rodeo?"

"What about it?"

His deliberate obtuseness grated on her nerves. She gritted her teeth. "Is your bad leg the rodeo's big loss as well?"

"No." He looked her straight in the eye.

She realized, with no small measure of guilt, that she'd been hoping for a different answer.

"The rodeo circuit isn't going to miss me one bit. I'm just another fair-to-middling cowboy used up too fast and tossed to the side of the road."

"So you're saying that you can't go back to the circuit?" She edged forward, holding her breath as if something monumental hinged on his reply.

"Oh, I can go back all right."

She exhaled in a long whoosh.

"I can't ever ride professionally again, but I can go back. Provided I can pay the admission price."

"Why wouldn't you?"

"I just told you. I'm out of the only work I was ever successful at, and my life savings are tied up in a certain dude ranch." He folded his hands together. "I'd consider selling off my belongings, but all I've got are the things I have with me at the ranch and a few items in a storage unit in Denver. I don't even have a home."

"Yes, you do."

Clint jerked his head up at the sound of her soft voice.

She swallowed hard and met his steady gaze.

In the bathroom the gushing shower spray stopped.

If she had something to say to this man, she had to say it now. Her heart raced, her stomach fluttered.

"Nina, I don't think that's—" He sighed and spread his hands. "Look at me, gal, I'm just a raggedy ol' cowboy, not good for anything anymore."

She bit her lip, she could not look at him. Her gaze dipped and glanced off the pile of pictures Alex had drawn. The top piece of childish artwork made her catch her breath.

A tall man in a cowboy hat stood next to a smaller figure. Both smiled up at her above a lopsided caption that read: "If you can't be my dad, I'm glad you're my friend."

Tears trembled along her lashes, but she sniffled and blinked them back.

"You want to know what you're good for, Clint?" She reached out to hand him the picture.

He took it reluctantly at first, then stared at it as if it were a blueprint to happiness.

"You're good for Alex, Clint." She wet her lips and angled her chin up. "And for me."

"Are you trying to say you think I just might be that father by faith after all?"

She gazed at him, feeling tears once again constricting her throat. She opened her mouth to speak, but at that moment Alex came bounding into the room.

"Are the fish ready yet?"

"Not yet." Clint stood with some effort and propped up the drawing on the mantel. He gave it one last look before turning to the boy and frowning. "Truth is, Alex, your mom and I were just about to flip a coin to see—"

"To see which one of us cleans and which one of us cooks." Nina stood, aiming a clear-eyed gaze at Clint in hopes he'd read the underlying message in her words. "But that's really not necessary, Clint. You know, everyone on a ranch—or any successful cooperative type of relationship—has to do his job and trust others to do theirs.

"And?"

"And if you'll clean the fish, just like you volunteered to do earlier, I'll see if I can't cook them up to everyone's satisfaction."

170

She stepped up to him and put her hand out. "Deal?"

For a brief moment, she thought she saw pain in his eyes, but then it faded. He sighed, nodded, and took her hand in his warm grasp. "Deal."

They shook, then stood there for several weighty seconds looking at each other.

Do it. She swallowed. She'd just made an overture that might lead to who knew what. But now that Clint was not leaving, now that he had every reason to stay, a new vigor and boldness filled her like fresh water poured onto a wilted flower. She smiled and tugged lightly on his arm to bring him forward just enough for her to arch her feet, strain her neck, risk her heart, and give him a quick, sweet kiss on the cheek.

Chapter ELEVEN

Nina, I think you've reached the wrong conclusion." Clint shook his head, releasing the scent of shampoo from his freshly washed hair. Surely he could come up with a better opening line.

He stilled, listening quietly to try to gauge how much longer Nina would dawdle in putting Alex to bed in the next room.

"Story time's over, young man. Let's get to the prayers, and then it's lights out," he heard her say.

He didn't have much time to come up with the perfect lead into the serious discussion about why they could never be more than business partners.

Of course, up until this moment, he'd had plenty of time; all day, in fact. But it had never seemed to be the right time. What was he supposed to do? Blurt it out over breakfast? Holler it during their hike? Spill it while they laughed, watching Alex splash in the water? Dish it up with their cozy, quiet dinner?

"God bless Mama and Grammie and Paw-paw and Plinkey...." Alex's innocent blessings drifted through the thin walls.

Clint rubbed his hands over his face. Since the moment

Nina had said that he was good for Alex—and for her—and gave him that kiss on the cheek, chaste as it was, Clint hadn't found the time, or the nerve, to tell her the truth. He stared into the roaring fire, the only illumination in the dim cabin this evening. If only he could find the right words, a way to let her know the problem was his, not hers.

The easiest way to do that, he supposed, was to tell her the truth, the whole story of Jamie and Mark and the life he had chosen to lead since losing them. But somehow he could not do that. If Nina knew, if he spoke their names aloud to her, then everything would come crashing in around him. He would have to face things he'd grown too comfortable leaving hidden away.

"And God bless Clint."

Alex's quiet plea ripped at Clint's gut.

He was in a business relationship with Nina, and he had been a role model for her son. How could he turn to her and admit what a miserable failure he'd been as a husband and father and still maintain any kind of respect? He gritted his teeth and sighed.

"Nina," he whispered, sounding out another approach, "I am so sorry if I've said or done anything to make you believe…"

"Go to sleep, sweetheart. You know Clint has a big day planned for us tomorrow," Nina cooed from the other room.

Clint laid his head back against the carved wooden frame of the couch and sighed. What hadn't he done to lead her to this conclusion? He'd offered, no, *imposed* his opinions about every aspect of the ranch, insisted they go to church together, all but took her son under his wing, and rushed in to rescue her dream business at great personal expense. He'd all but begged her to stay up here with him awhile longer. And he'd kissed her pretty, paint-smudged lips.

The memory of that kiss drew his attention to the flames leaping in the fireplace. Nothing he'd done in a decade had felt that natural, that good, that special—and so wrong.

It was wrong to mislead them both, to allow them to think for even an instant that they could form a loving bond. Still, he couldn't help thinking of that kiss often. He figured that memory, and all the memories of Nina and Alex and his time here with them, would linger long after he'd moved on. Those memories would warm many a lonely night in the years to come.

"Mesmerizing, isn't it?"

Clint tore his gaze from the fire to see Nina's face basked in the golden light.

"Yes," he answered, but he wasn't talking about the fire.

"The weather's probably not cool enough for it." She lowered herself to the floor in front of the stone hearth. "But since we've built it up this much, I thought it might be nice to keep it going."

She looked at him, and her eyes told him that she wasn't talking about the fire anymore, either. "At least for a little while longer."

"Nina—"

"Don't, Clint." She bowed her head. "Don't say it yet. We've had such a lovely day, and it was so nice to pretend—and I realize now it was just pretend—that we could be a family."

He shook his head. He could not look at her. "I never meant to hurt you, you know."

"I know."

The serenity of her whispered reply slashed at his heart, unleashing wave upon wave of guilt and remorse. All day his emotions had been raging and subsiding. They would surface to tighten his throat or cause a deep, dull stabbing in his chest before he reined them in again.

Now, sitting half in shadow, with so much he wanted to say,

he felt so helpless over their circumstances that the long-buried pain rose once again. He swallowed but could not suppress the cold lump swelling in his chest. He shut his eyes and gripped his hand into a powerful fist.

His words came strained and hushed, but once they began, they poured out for her, without any effort or thought from him. "If I had the power, I'd take back everything. You know that, don't you?"

"Clint, I—"

"I never wanted to involve you, never wanted to get too close and let you think that I was the kind of man who could be a husband or father. I can't. I won't."

He pushed his hand through his hair, his face down. "I was wrong. Wrong to stay here once I knew the kind of woman you were, once I knew about your son. It was weak and selfish of me to stay."

"No, Clint..."

"Yes!" He pounded his fist on his knee and welcomed the distraction of the immediate, piercing pain jolting through his injured leg. He drew in a sharp breath and looked up into the hissing flames. "I'm a selfish and weak man, Jamie. If I wasn't, I'd have never hurt you and Mark the way I have, all for my own—"

"Clint, stop. Go back a minute." She crept toward him on her knees over the shag carpet, forcing him to meet her gaze. "Who is Jamie? Who is Mark?"

He blinked, trying to make himself understand how Nina knew those names.

"You called me Jamie just now," she said, as if she knew his thoughts. "And you said you'd never have hurt Jamie and Mark. Clint, who are Jamie and Mark?"

Cool tears bathed his eyes but not one dared to fall. He clenched his jaw, and somehow through the fog of his whirlwind of emotions, he made the quiet, unemotional reply, "Jamie and Mark are my wife and son."

"You're...you're m-married?" Nina put her hand to her head, trying to make sense of all the strange things she was hearing and feeling.

"Was." He narrowed his eyes at her, hitting the single word hard. "I *was* married. I lost my wife and son five years ago."

"Oh, Clint, I didn't know." She reached out to place one hand on his knee.

He shrugged. "I didn't tell you."

"That's how you knew so much about kids and—"

He brushed her hand away. "That's how I know I can never be the kind of man you and Alex need."

She curled her fingers against her chest, pressing her lips together and hearing only her thudding heart. "I don't believe that."

He clenched and unclenched his hand. He made several halting, restless movements, making the sagging sofa creak and groan. "You don't have to believe it, Nina, but it's true."

"It's not true. The man I've known this past month is neither selfish nor weak," she protested.

He snorted his disagreement.

"Would a selfish man have helped me the way you have?" She knew she was pushing him, perhaps too far, but she couldn't sit here and let him think these harsh things about himself. "Would he have the kind of patience you've had with Alex?"

"He might, if he had his reasons."

"Clint, don't say things like that. It makes you sound so—"

"Honest?" He sneered.

She had no idea what to say to that.

"Because that's what it is, Nina. Honesty." The deep red-orange light of the fire flickered in his eyes. "I'm not just trying

177

to play on your sympathies when I say this." He paused. "My wife and son would be alive today if I hadn't put my own needs and desires ahead of the family."

She felt her head shake in disbelief. Her teeth pressed against her lower lip, but she said nothing to contradict him.

"I had just won my first big championship and was so full of myself." He bowed his head. "I wanted to go on to another rodeo. I told Jamie it was because I'd finally gotten my act together. I was going to begin earning serious money, and I wanted to start right away. We'd done without for so long I said I couldn't wait to afford great things for my family."

"That hardly sounds selfish."

He huffed out a grim laugh. "What I really wanted was to show off, to feel the thrill of the crowd again. I was only thinking of myself. Jamie asked me not to go. We argued."

Nina looked away, unable to look at the anguish in Clint's eyes.

"I took off anyway, figuring we'd settle it all later. But Jamie, she was like a dog with a bone. When something really mattered to her, she just couldn't let it go." He cocked his head, his voice barely a whisper. "You remind me of her a lot in that way."

"I do?" She hugged her knees to her chest. Somehow, this tidbit of information comforted her.

"Yes, and that should have been enough to run me off the ranch that very first night."

"Oh." Her spirits fell.

He pinched at an invisible speck of lint on his jeans and flicked it away. "I left for that rodeo and Jamie took off after me with Mark in the car. They were in a head-on collision with a car whose driver had fallen asleep."

"I'm so sorry," she murmured.

He nodded. "Me, too."

"But, Clint, surely you can't blame yourself for that. It was an accident."

"I don't blame myself for the accident. I blame myself for not being the kind of man my family could count on."

"You were going to earn money for them...." Her argument faded under his cool gaze.

"Don't you get it, Nina? It's my fault she felt she had to come after me, because she couldn't trust that I was the kind of man who would always come back." He hung his head. "I was too self-involved, too unable to give of myself. She suspected that this one more rodeo would turn into two, then three, then who knew how many before I came back."

"You'd have come back." She laid her hand on the cushion beside him.

"I wish I could believe that, but I'm not one hundred percent sure." He lifted his face to the firelight. "And nothing I've done since then has made me think differently of myself."

"I think differently. I'd trust you to come back, and so would Alex."

"Nina, much as I appreciate your confidence in me, I think it may be misplaced." He folded his hands, then unfolded them. "I've spent a decade on the rodeo circuit, avoiding commitment, burying my feelings, hiding from the past. Nothing about any of that makes me feel like a changed man."

"Not even your faith?"

He smiled. "A few weeks ago, I'd have asked what my faith has to do with any of this."

"But now?"

"But now I've met a certain little boy who made me wonder how I could hang on so steadfastly to a heart that I'd supposedly given to the Lord."

Nina sighed. That was the first optimistic statement she'd heard this evening. "So you have changed."

"I was raised in the church, Nina. I gave my life to the Lord as a teenager. I won't pretend I haven't faltered or that I haven't wrestled with issues of faith and decided to take the easy way out."

She scanned his earnest features, her heart heavy with anxiety over his unvarnished revelations.

"But I counted myself a Christian the day I chose the rodeo over my family, the day I drove off not sure when, or if, I'd return." He stretched his leg out and jiggled it, wincing.

"What are you saying, Clint?"

"I'm saying that I haven't changed at all. I'm still the same flawed man I was then. I wish you could see that."

"We're all flawed, Clint. That's why we all need to be forgiven." She drew her shoulders up. "I just wish you could see beyond the flaws."

He shook his head, his gaze directed downward. "I'm afraid of what I'd find."

"Maybe that's because you'd find a man who has begun to question his old way of thinking."

He jerked his head up to meet her eyes. His breathing stayed even, his eyes searching. Slowly, a chuckle rose from his chest. His mouth quirked up on one side. "Like a dog with a bone."

"Well?"

He groaned and laughed at the same time. "Okay. Okay, Nina. I'll admit I'm finding it very difficult to hang on to all the blame and to keep myself closed off. But that doesn't make me a good risk for a relationship."

She mimicked his grin. "It's a start."

"Nina, I don't want to get your hopes up that anything can really happen between us." He put his hand beneath her chin.

His touch sent a shiver through her, despite his words of denial. She wet her lips and inhaled the mingled scents of wood smoke in the air and soap on his skin. Her pulse raced.

The fire flared, popping and sizzling in the hushed atmosphere of the cabin.

"Don't worry about me, Clint. Whatever does or does not happen between us, I can handle it."

"Maybe you can, but what about Alex? Whatever our relationship is, we have to protect him."

"Oh, I agree. I don't want Alex to see or hear anything that might feed his longing to bring us together as a family." She pushed up from the floor. "And speaking of my son, I'd better go check in on him."

She took one step, realizing too late her foot had fallen asleep. It came down on the floor at an awkward angle. Her ankle turned. She flailed her arms to help regain her balance, but the wrenching pain in her ankle disabled her. With ungainly momentum, she twisted herself around and plopped down on the sofa at his side.

The unstable sofa legs squawked. The frame wobbled. The yellow, eagle-patterned cushions sighed but took her sudden weight with apparent ease. Nina hesitated, her breath trapped in her lungs.

Clint studied her, waiting.

The sofa settled.

Their gazes held.

The fire crackled, throwing its romantic glow over them. She sat so close to him she could see the light dancing in his pupils, feel the warmth, not from the fire, but from him, enveloping her. She tipped her head, and without thinking, wet her lips.

His eyes shifted and she felt his gaze skim her mouth.

She exhaled, slowly.

He did the same.

Then the cushions caved in.

"Whoa!" Clint clutched at her arm to keep her from tumbling on top of him.

Her cheek brushed against the crisp cotton of his shirt, then flattened against the solid wall of his muscular chest. She twined her arms around him to try to push herself upright, but before she could make herself move an inch, a soft sound drew her attention.

"Alex?" Clint said as he tried to help her sit up again.

Nina would have called her son's name as well, but she had a mouth full of shirt pocket.

"Alex? That you, pal?"

Another muted sound came from the other room and then all was silent.

Nina shoved herself away from Clint and struggled up from the bottomed-out couch.

Her ankle pulsed with pain, but she stood tall on it, her head held high. "As I was saying, I guess I'd better go check on Alex. Then, I think, I'll go to bed myself. We've had a very...eventful day."

Clint merely nodded.

"Good night," she said, hobbling toward the bedroom, hoping with every step that he'd at least call out a good night. Something, anything, to make the connection with her again, to give her something to dream on, something to hope.

Clint said nothing.

911.

Nina awakened to find the universal code for an emergency flashing on her pager. While Clint fixed Alex his breakfast, she called the ranch, then joined them, her face pale.

Her putting-on-a-brave-face-for-Alex routine hardly fooled Clint. He knew that behind the taut smile and clipped laughter,

Nina was near panic. After sending Alex off on an errand to fetch something from his truck, Clint coaxed the reason out of her: her in-laws had already arrived at the ranch.

After he convinced her she could not afford the luxury of hyperventilating, Clint helped her collect their things. He hustled Alex into the car, intending to drive them both back. But Nina was too quick. She pounced into the driver's seat in the time it took him to buckle the boy up and drove away without looking back.

The idea of her driving under this level of emotional stress frightened Clint, frightened him more than he ever wanted to be frightened again. He had no time to waste. He had to follow her.

His heart thudded faster and harder when his tires spun in the muddy road. He gritted his teeth and offered a brief, sincere prayer. "Not again, Lord. Protect her and the boy. And please, let me catch up with her so that she won't face her in-laws alone. Let me show her that she can count on me to stand by her side in this, if not forever."

As the back road converged with the main one that wound downward to Jackson's Butte, he spotted her taillights, and his breathing eased.

In front of the ranch house, she had hardly slid from behind the wheel when his truck rolled to a stop next to her.

"Nina, wait," he called above the sound of both their doors slamming.

She swung her head to face him, the sunlight bouncing off her gleaming hair.

Dust kicked up from the gravel crunching under his boots as he came around to block her path. "You need to take a few seconds to compose yourself before you go in there and face them."

She stole a sidelong glance at the building, gnawing on the edge of a fingernail.

"Just stop a minute." He held his hand up. "Close your eyes."

She obeyed.

"Take a deep breath."

She gulped in the fresh morning air.

"And—"

Wham.

"Grammie! Paw-paw! I've got so much stuff to tell you!"

Nina's eyes flew open, and she nearly choked on her gasp of surprise.

Clint flinched. He'd blown it now. They both watched helplessly as Alex took off sprinting toward the front porch where his grandparents stood.

"Compose myself?" She pushed Clint aside to chase after her son. "Thanks to your little delaying tactic, the only thing I'll be composing is an apology. Thanks for nothing, Cooper."

Chapter TWELVE

"G rammie! Paw-paw! Guess what? I got my dad!" Alex waved his hands in the air. His feet had barely hit the steps when he flung himself at his grandparents. "I got a new dad!"

"Alex, no!" Nina fisted her hands against her temples. This could not be happening. Her legs felt as if they'd been turned to rubber as she raced after her blabbermouth of a child. Her every footfall pounded slower and slower on the uneven ground, jarring her through to her clenched teeth. Ahead she saw Alex's grandfather lift the boy into the air. His grandmother stretched up on tiptoe to plant a kiss on the boy's round cheek.

"I'll bet you've grown a foot since you left us," Grammie Jackson said.

"And he's gotten heavier, too." Paw-paw Jackson hoisted the boy high against his chest. "What are they feeding you out here? Beefsteak and boulders?"

Alex giggled, his head shaking. "We eat bacon and eggs for breakfast now, except at the cabin we had fish!"

"Fish?" Grammie's whole face wrinkled in worry.

"Yep. Me and Clint caught 'em ourselves, and Mama fried 'em up."

"Is that so? You and your mama and this—what did you say his name was?"

"Clint."

"Clint." Paw-paw nodded as if making a mental note. "And the three of you were off at this cabin together?"

Nina felt her heart sink like a water balloon dropped from a skyscraper. Any second now she expected to hear a horrific *splat* fill her ears, followed by the thud of her body keeling over in a dead faint. What she heard instead was Clint coming up behind her. And she realized she'd come to a halt a few steps away from the porch.

"We didn't go up there together; we got stuck together by a rainstorm," Alex explained.

"Oh, I see," said Paw-paw.

"And then Clint wanted to show me how to catch fish and I was really good at it and then Mama said 'who's going to clean them?' and I thought she meant give them a bath and…" The child's words rushed out so fast, they tumbled over each other trying to get out of his mouth.

Nina blinked. She stole the few moments while Alex chattered to try to put the scene in focus.

Mr. and Mrs. Jackson seemed calm. That was a good sign. Alex continued regaling them with his story, a virtual poster child for the easygoing ranch life. Also good. She no longer felt like fainting—a small comfort, if nothing else. And Clint—

Clint placed his hand on her arm, no doubt a sign of support and solidarity. He stood so close she could hear his breath in her ear, feel his protective attitude toward her and Alex go up like a force field around them. That was neither a comfort nor a good sign.

At least Alex hadn't said the dreaded *D* word again.

"And then we made another fire and I got sleepy and Mama made me go to bed, except that I didn't get a chance to tell Clint good night and so I woked up again and I got up and went out to tell him and then I saw him and Mama hugging on the couch and I sneaked back real quick so they wouldn't get mad that I was out of bed—" Alex drew in a huge breath through his mouth. "And that's how I knew I was gonna get what I prayed for the very first night we stayed here!"

"And what was that, son?" Paw-paw asked.

The word 'no' formed on Nina's lips, but her voice failed as Alex grinned at his grandparents and proclaimed with pride and excitement, "A new dad, Paw-paw. Clint's going to be my new daddy."

She had to stop this. She had to find a way to defuse the anger and confusion she expected to meet her like a wall when she reached that porch. Otherwise, she might lose everything. If they thought for one moment that they had financed her trip out here just to have her take up with a man—

Nina could not imagine how devastated they would be. Their one goal in life seemed to be to preserve the memory of their lost son for Alex, to keep the boy's father alive in his mind. They would not take lightly the notion that their grandson wanted to call another man Dad.

She slipped her arm away from Clint's grasp and charged up the stairs and onto the porch.

"Oh, now Alex, honey, don't go telling wild tales to Grammie and Paw-paw." She practically peeled Alex out of the older man's hands. "Now, why don't you run inside and—"

"I can't go now, Mama, I didn't even tell them about how we're going to go back to the cabin when we're a real family or about Plinkey or nothing."

"Plinkey?" Grammie glanced from Nina to her bewildered, gray-haired husband.

Paw-paw scowled. "Just who is Plinkey, and what's all this about—"

"Plinkey is the boy's pony." Clint stepped up, his hands on his hips, his hat tipped back to reveal his face.

"I see." Paw-paw looked down the length of his nose at Clint, something he was only able to do since Clint stood on the lowest step. "And who might you be?"

"That's Clint Cooper. He's my new—"

"I have a great idea." Nina clapped her hands together to cut off another of Alex's announcements. "Alex, why don't you and Clint go out to the barn, saddle up Plinkey, and then you can ride him out and show him to your grandparents?"

"Okay!" Alex leaped in the air.

"Why doesn't Alex just bring the pony out by his lead?" Clint plunked one booted foot on the next step up, bringing him closer behind Nina. "That way I can stay here and help you sort through things with Mr. and Mrs. Jackson."

"Please, Clint, I'd rather handle this alone."

"But, Nina, I think it would go much smoother with me here to back you up." His eyes shone with a determined light.

"The last thing I need right now is an argument from you," she whispered. "Please, just take Alex and let me deal with this."

"I'll do it. But I'm doing it under protest."

Nina smiled. "Aw, you're just afraid that after being away for two days that Shetland will have worked up a powerful appetite for a mouthful of rump roast."

"Thanks for reminding me not to turn my back on the beastie." He swung his arm out toward Alex. "Okay, pal, let's go see if we can wrastle a saddle onto that set of steel jaws in horsehide."

They started off.

"Wait one moment, young man—uh, Mr. Cooper." Paw-

paw held up one hand.

They paused and Clint glanced over his shoulder. "I beg your pardon, sir?"

"I said wait right there."

Nina's heart stopped. She'd hoped to get Clint and Alex on their way before the fireworks began, before she found herself upbraided for her behavior, for dishonoring the memory of her late husband. Now, it seemed that was not to be. Mr. Jackson was going to make them all stay and suffer through the humiliation of her explanation for what appeared to be an inexcusable situation.

"Why are you running off?" Paw-paw asked.

"He's going to help Alex saddle his pony," Nina said, her desperation giving her words a breathless quality. "You two run along now and get Plinkey. Grammie and Paw-paw and I want to have a little talk."

"Yes, ma'am, we have to have a talk," Paw-paw boomed.

Nina felt ice water begin to seep through her veins.

"But we can't very well have that talk without this young man present."

"We can't?" Nina choked out.

"Of course not, dear." Grammie gave her an affectionate hug. "If this young man is going to be our precious grandson's new father, we most certainly want to take all the time we can to get to know him."

Nina's entire face wrinkled in confusion. She cocked her head and gaped at her in-laws, wondering if their bodies had suddenly been invaded by pod people. She blinked to try to get the whirlwind in her brain to settle down, placed her hands on her hips, and said the single most eloquent thing that came to mind. "Huh?"

"This is just great." Clint knocked a cabinet door closed with his knee, then yanked open another. He and Nina had managed to excuse themselves to get refreshments while the Jacksons waited patiently on the leather couch in the lobby for their return. "I come chasing after you, half out of my head with worry that your state of mind might affect your driving, and what do I get for it?"

"Coffee?" She flashed a steaming pot of the black brew at him.

He shook his head to decline.

"I get mistaken for an interloping soon-to-be stepdad." He plucked up the delicate glass vase Nina had asked him to find, then shut the cabinet with a sturdy wham. "Now I know how an innocent man feels when he's standing on the gallows and suddenly the floor falls out from under him."

"My, how you do flatter a girl with your analogies." She snatched the vase away and plunked it down on a serving tray. "I don't think I've ever had a man compare a relationship with me to a dead man's drop before."

"That's not how I meant it and you know it."

"Yes, that's right, you've given me plenty of reasons to know you didn't mean that as an insult." She arranged the coffee cups and a flat basket filled with fruit, crackers, cheeses, and cookies on the large tray. She then peered out the back window to see if Alex was coming with the flowers she'd asked him to pick.

Daylight poured over her cheeks and nose, and for the first time, Clint realized that she had dark circles beneath her eyes. This whole mess had been hard on her, and it showed in her sad expression, in the weariness that never quite left her features anymore. Trying to start this ranch, being a good mom, and dealing with the emotional havoc his presence brought had taken its toll. Did he need any further proof that he was no good for Nina and Alex?

The best thing for him to do, he decided, was to let her handle this in her own way. His job from now until her in-laws left was to keep his mouth shut and go along with whatever she said or did. She would get no trouble from him; no arguments, no power struggles.

"I'm sorry I snapped at you, Clint." Her lashes dipped, she sighed, and then turned her shoulders toward him, still avoiding his gaze. "And I'm sorry you got caught up in all this nonsense when all you wanted to do was help."

He'd wanted a great deal more, he thought as he studied her sweet face. That offered undeniable evidence to him that we don't always want what's best for us—or for those we love.

Love? Where did that come from, he wondered, his pulse quickening. Could it be possible that he really loved Nina? *Loved* her?

What should have been a joyous revelation weighed heavy on his mind. His chest ached. His gaze could not quite settle on any one thing in the room, especially Nina's face. Confronting his feelings only made things worse—one hundred times worse, he realized. Not only was it harder for him to do the right thing, but now knowing he loved Nina made it all the more imperative that he do just that.

He had to break away from Nina and Alex for their own sakes. He swallowed and suddenly realized she'd been staring at him, probably waiting for some response.

He pushed his hair back off his forehead. "Just forget it, Nina."

"No, I can't forget it, Clint." She moved around him so that he had to meet her gaze. "I'll never forget what you've done for us."

"Nina, don't," he croaked.

"Don't what?"

"Don't try to build me up into something I'm not." He rested one hand on her shoulder. "I'm just a guy who came to do a job, and hopefully that's what I've done."

"You're much more than that to me and you know it." She placed her hand on top of his.

"If I am, it's not by my choice." He stepped back.

"What do you mean, Clint?"

"What do you think I mean?"

"Well, it sounds like you believe you've been ramrodded."

He chuckled without any amusement. "And you're acting like you think I haven't been."

"Nobody forced you to do any of the things you've done around here," she argued, a fire stirring in her eyes that had not been there before.

Good. Fight back, Nina. Fight your way out of wanting anything from me but the sight of my taillights as I drive away.

"Nobody forced me, that's true." He crossed his arms over his chest and threw his shoulders back, the epitome of cowboy cockiness. "But we can't say nobody coerced me, now can we?"

"What?"

That's it, he urged her silently, *get mad.* "You heard what I said."

"Are you implying that I—?" She thumped her thumb against her breastbone.

"And don't forget Alex," he goaded.

"Alex?"

"Sure, Alex. Isn't he the one who started this whole campaign to rope good ol' Clint into becoming resident dude ranch dad?"

"How dare you suggest that my son used subterfuge to try to trap you into becoming his father. How could you think he could be so—so—so conniving?"

"Says the mother of the kid who informed the staff that I was his dad."

She narrowed her eyes at him, her cheeks taking on a scarlet glow.

He continued to tick off examples one by one on his fingers. "Let's see, the kid also ran off to tell his Sunday-school teacher and his grandparents the same news. For all we know, it's posted on the Internet."

"Whatever Alex may or may not have done, he did it in innocence."

"Maybe, but who put him up to it? That's what I want to know."

She stabbed her thumb to her chest again. "Me?"

"Ah," he said, rubbing his hands together. "A confession."

"A confession?" she squawked. "Listen, my friend, the only thing I want to confess to is being totally naive about you. I guess I let my judgment get clouded by feelings of gratitude and—and—"

Don't say it, he commanded with a look.

"Friendship," she finished.

Why did it disappoint him that she didn't mention some stronger emotion?

"And imagine, I honestly thought we were starting to make some kind of connection." She shook her head. "And all that time, you suspected me of prompting my child to trick you into becoming part of our family."

There was no way he could lie to her, tell her he had thought that when it was the furthest thing from the truth. So he found a noncommittal way to answer her question. "Hey, if the direct approach doesn't work, it's no shame to try to go around the back way."

Her eyes narrowed to slits, her hands to fists at her sides. "Ooh, I'd love to go around your back way—and boot you right off my ranch."

"Except you can't do that because it's also my ranch."

She sniffed. "Isn't that convenient?"

"For whom?"

"How about for a man who has no home of his own to go back to and an ego so big it would take a thousand acres of real estate to contain it?"

"There aren't enough acres in all of Colorado, sister."

She arched an eyebrow. "To hold your ego?"

"To hold the two of us," he snarled.

"If you feel that way, then maybe you should become an absentee landlord."

"Sounds like a pretty good idea to me." What choice did he have? It was either get out or dive in with both feet. "As soon as we get this little mix-up straightened out with your in-laws, I'm out of here."

"Oh, well don't let that stop you. I can handle my in-laws myself."

"Uh-uh. Those people are, until we can make arrangements otherwise, my business partners, too. I want in on this little powwow with Grammie and Paw-paw."

"Okay, if that's the way you want it. But let's get to it and get it over with. The sooner it's done, the sooner you're out of here."

"Fine."

"Fine."

Nina grabbed up the tray of coffee and snacks and spun away from him. "Am I ever sorry I didn't just leave you in that cabin and come back here where I belong."

"That makes two of us. Luckily, we'll never go up there again." He took one step, then stumbled against her still body.

She let out a quiet *oomph.*

"Now what?" Clint grumbled. One glance over her shoulder told him what had brought her to a halt.

There, in the doorway, stood a little towheaded boy, a handful of scraggly flowers clutched in one fist.

"Are those for Grammie?" Nina asked softly, as if Alex had walked in on them standing in the kitchen amicably discussing the weather.

He nodded, his eyes serious.

The sight tugged at Clint's already raw emotions.

"Why don't you put them in the vase, okay?" She bent at the knees to lower the tray.

Alex poked the bedraggled stems into the throat of the glistening vase.

"Isn't that pretty?" she asked.

Alex nodded again.

"Now, Clint and I are going to go in and talk with Grammie and Paw-paw. There are some cookies on the counter and some crackers and cheese and fruit. Why don't you pick something and have a little snack. Would you like that, honey?"

He nodded a third time.

"Okay." She straightened, gave a quick peek over her shoulder at Clint, then led the way toward the door.

Clint followed, feeling as if he were dragging his heart behind him as they went.

"Mama?"

They both turned.

Alex stuffed a handful of grapes into his shirt pocket, then snatched up two stacks of chocolate chip cookies. "Can I go out and ride Plinkey?"

Nina's face brightened. "Sure, sweetie, but make sure you get someone on staff to put the saddle on. And before you start riding, make sure the gate that leads to the trails is closed off so you can keep Plinkey inside the front area, okay?"

"I'll get a grown-up to put the saddle on." Alex nodded, then folded the cookies with some crackers and cheese into a napkin and took an apple. "Thanks, Mama."

"Have fun, sweetie." Nina turned and headed through the door, pausing only long enough to square her shoulders in obvious preparation for facing her in-laws.

"Would you stop it?" The naked anxiety of Nina's tone stood out in the quiet of the room like the sour twang of a poorly tuned guitar.

The Jacksons and Clint all snapped their heads up at the same time. Grammie's coffee cup tottered on the saucer in her hand. Paw-paw's mouth hung open, the charming story he'd been sharing with Clint cut off before its conclusion. The three of them, sitting in casual comfort in an intimate semicircle with Clint's chair pushed close to the couch, simply stared up at her.

"Stop what?" Clint asked, his hands clasped between his knees.

"Stop being so…cozy."

"Cozy?" Clint curled his lip up. "I've been called a lot of things, Nina, several of them by you, but never cozy."

Paw-paw muffled a laugh.

Grammie slapped at his knee to reprimand him.

"I thought you'd be pleased that Henry and I are getting on so famously with your new young man, Nina, dear," Grammie said, blinking her big, clear eyes.

"He is not my young man," Nina protested. "He's my ranch foreman."

"And business partner," Clint added.

"For the time being," she reminded him. How, oh how, would she ever present a picture of maturity and confidence with Clint undermining her efforts to downplay his role?

Nina tugged at the waistband of her jeans, smoothing down the soft T-shirt over her churning stomach.

"I don't understand, dear." Grammie placed her cup and saucer on the end table beside the couch. "Alex said—"

Nina held up her hand. "Alex is a little boy who thinks that because Clint showed up right after he prayed for a new father that Clint must be that new father."

"That's not such a far-fetched conclusion, you know," Paw-paw muttered. "The Lord works in mysterious ways, and he does answer prayer, don't you think?"

"Yes, of course." Nina started to cross her arms, then stopped and let them fall to her sides.

"As a matter of fact, we've been praying for just that thing as well." Grammie cocked her head. "For God to provide you with a husband and Alex with a new father."

"You have?" Nina's knees buckled at the uncharacteristic comment, but she managed to stay on her feet.

"Of course we have." Paw-paw leaned back, scowling. Clearly, it insulted him that she might think otherwise.

"We only want what's best for you and Alex, dear." Grammie's voice rang soft and pleasant in the tense atmosphere. "We know that a young boy needs a role model, a man to look up to, someone to guide him into manhood."

The chair leg scraped the tile floor as Clint shifted in his seat.

Grammie did not seem to notice his discomfort about the topic. "And as for you, well, we don't want you to be alone forever."

"You don't?" She sank into a chair facing her in-laws.

"Mercy, no, dear." Grammie's whole face crinkled in laughter. "You're still a young woman. That's why we agreed to loan you the money to help finance this big move."

"Because I'm still young?" She shook her head, but that didn't jar things into focus.

"Yes." Paw-paw frowned. "You're young and it was long past time for you to get on with your life, as much for Alex's sake as your own."

"You never would have done that with us peeking over your shoulder day in and day out."

"Peeking over my shoulder?" She could not help but smile at the understatement. "In all honesty, Grammie and Paw-paw, you did a little bit more than just peek. I felt as if you never approved of anything I did, that you've always questioned the way I raise Alex. Why this sudden change of heart?"

Paw-paw's features softened. "Because we know now that you have this fine, upstanding young man to help you—with your business and with Alex."

Nina's throat closed in a mix of panic and anger, straining her voice as she said, "But you hardly know this man. And now you're saying this stranger is better equipped to raise Alex than I am?"

"Slow down, Nina." Clint brought his hand over so that his fingertips brushed her knee. "He did not say that."

She glared at Clint.

"No, dear." Grammie rushed to intervene. "You misunderstand. We don't have any doubts about your abilities as a mother or as a businesswoman."

Nina crossed her arms. "You'd just feel better if someone else was helping."

"Exactly." Grammie beamed at her.

"Exactly," Nina muttered, rolling her eyes.

"I don't care what the modern thinking is, young lady." Paw-paw edged forward on the couch. "You can't have it all—at least not all at once. You've got a good thing in this dude ranch, and you've done a terrific job with Alex. You deserve a little help with them both."

"That's why Henry and I were always so close to lend our support and expertise," Grammie added, beaming.

"Support and expertise?" Nina sighed, able to relax for the first time in years around her in-laws. "That's what you call it?"

"Yes." Grammie blinked. "What would you call it, dear?"

Nina pressed her lips together. She eyed Clint, who kicked up his ankle to rest on his knee and cast her a beguiling grin.

"Meddling?" Grammie suggested when Nina did not answer.

"Oh, no…well, yes." Nina laughed. "Yes, I believe I may have used that term a time or two."

"We thought so."

"I didn't think so," Paw-paw objected.

"You would have if you ever once took the time to listen to me, Henry."

The older man took the scolding in good humor, and Nina had to pause and consider. Could she have misinterpreted the Jacksons' behavior after Wayne's death? The thought of her late husband brought a new question to mind.

"I really appreciate everything you've tried to do for me, especially looking at it in this new light." She twisted her hands together in her lap. "But there's one more thing I just have to ask—what about Wayne?"

Grammie's eyes grew misty.

Paw-paw coughed into his fisted hand. "What about Wayne?"

"You don't feel my finding someone new and Alex calling another man Daddy would be a disservice to his memory?"

"Just the opposite." Paw-paw reached out his hand to take Grammie's. "We know you had a good marriage; that you

199

would want to go on and find love again is a testament to that. And Alex—what better tribute could we wish for our son than to know his son has a good role model, a new father who loves him and you?"

Nina clenched her teeth. She dared not look at Clint as she told her in-laws the truth—that Clint neither loved her nor would he become Alex's father.

"Grammie, Paw-paw, first I have to apologize for my harsh judgment of your actions."

"That's all right, dear."

"Put it out of your mind." Paw-paw waved it off. "In fact, this whole conversation is getting a bit weighty for my tastes. What do you say we find out what little Alex is up to?"

"Yes, let's." Grammie tapped Paw-paw on the knee.

He rose slowly, then turned to offer her his hand and help her from the couch.

"Wait, I have something more to say." Nina stood, flashed Clint a pleading look, then cupped Grammie's elbow to steady her as she stepped between the chair and sofa.

Grammie sighed. "Honestly, dear, I don't think I can concentrate on another syllable."

"Save the jabbering for later," Paw-paw said. "Right now we just want to enjoy our grandson."

"I really think you need to hear Nina out, Mr. and Mrs. Jackson." Clint also straightened up from his chair. "You see, Alex may have given you the wrong impression about me."

"Pish-tosh." Paw-paw opened the front door and held it for Grammie. "Never could abide a man with too much modesty, son. We appreciate that the boy's perception may be colored with a child's admiration, but we can see you're a fine man."

"And that you love our Nina," Grammie added, as she stepped across the threshold.

Nina gulped, but that did not dissipate her humiliation at

the simplistic view Grammie had of the situation. She started to deny the very notion, but the soft murmur of Clint, perhaps speaking to himself, caught her up short.

"You can see that, can you? I had no idea it was so obvious."

She spun around to confront him, to demand that he explain himself, as hope and fear warred in her heart. But before she could get a single sound from her lips, Grammie's voice interrupted.

"Nina? Nina, dear? Where is Alex?"

"He's right out front, riding his Shetland pony." She kept her gaze fixed on Clint's face. She wet her lips to speak to him and again Grammie's voice distracted her.

"No, he's not, dear."

Nina gritted her teeth and gave Clint what she prayed he'd interpret as an I'm-not-through-with-you-yet look, then hurried to the door to deal with Grammie's confusion.

"Alex!" she called.

The wind whipped at the dirt and grass in the open area between the barn and main building.

"Alex?"

A horse whinnied. Nina moved out to the porch steps to get a better look. Only a staff member grooming a trail pony came into sight. She swept her gaze over the familiar scene, then stopped, feeling cold.

"Maybe he's in the barn," Clint said, wedging his way past her. "I'll go check."

"I have a feeling you're not going to find him there." Nina grabbed Clint's arm, and when he stopped, she used one look to direct his attention to a clue to Alex's disappearance.

"The gate to the riding trails is open," Clint murmured. "You don't think…?"

"Yes, I do." Nina did not want to seem like an alarmist, but she could not sugarcoat her anxiety. The expression on Alex's face when he'd walked in on Clint and her arguing in the kitchen haunted her. Hurt and confused, a young boy like Alex might just try something foolish.

"What does that mean, dear?" Grammie tugged at Nina's shirtsleeve, her finger pointing at the open gate.

Nina nipped at her thumbnail and whispered, "It means that we have literally miles of riding trails out there, and Alex could be anywhere on them."

Chapter
THIRTEEN

G rammie and Paw-paw, you stay put and page me if Alex shows up back here. Ellen, you and the other staff members search the riding trails. Take my cellular phone and call here if you find him." Nina handed the small phone to the girl. "I'm going to drive up to the cabin."

"*I'm* going to drive up to the cabin. You're in no shape to drive anywhere." Clint had let her down when his harsh words had upset Alex enough to make the child run away. The least he could do was to find that boy before something unspeakable happened. Clint curled his hand around Nina's car keys.

She held onto them.

The cold metal dug into his palm as he tightened his grip. He could easily tear the keys from her, but he wanted her to give them to him. He needed to know she trusted him enough to do that.

"Will you stop worrying about my emotional state and my driving? I'm not Jamie," she whispered. "Don't treat me like I am."

He searched her face, a clutching in his chest as he responded in the same hoarse whisper, "I didn't ever ask Jamie for her keys."

His fingers closed over hers.

Her chin quivered, then she relinquished the keys and turned away from him. "We're wasting valuable time arguing. Let's get going."

Clint's teeth ground together as his truck jounced along the dirt road to the mountain cabins. Neither of them had a word to say. The air prickled with tension.

Clint watched out of the corner of his eye as Nina fidgeted beside him. First she tapped her foot against the floorboard. Then she gripped the armrest until her knuckles went white. Finally she leaned forward, straining against her seatbelt, as if she could spur the truck to go faster.

"Sit back, Nina, we'll get there." He touched her shoulder. "And we'll find Alex, safe and sound."

Nina took a deep breath, and as if his words had broken something in her, all her fears gushed forth. "Oh, Clint, what if he didn't go to the cabin? What if he went toward the main road and tried to get into town? What if someone came along and picked him up? What if—"

"It didn't happen that way, Nina."

"How do you know that? You can't know that."

"Yes, I can, Nina," he murmured.

"How?" she demanded. "How can you know?"

"Because I saw the look in his eyes."

Her face contorted in angry astonishment. "What?"

"When he walked in on our argument, I'd just said we'd never go to the cabin again. I saw the way he looked after that."

She jerked her head around so that she was staring out the windshield, her jaw clenched.

Clint watched her with lightning quick glances as he kept his concentration on the road. "Nina, how many times did you hear Alex talk about 'when we go back to the cabin again'?"

"As a real family."

"Hmm?"

"That's what he told my in-laws. We'd go back as a real family."

He could only nod and press his foot a little heavier against the gas pedal. How could he have let his old selfishness do this again? If he'd once thought about Nina and Alex before shooting his big mouth off, Alex would be parading Plinkey around in front of his grandparents right now.

If he hadn't threatened to leave, just as he'd left Jamie and Mark all those years ago...

His shoulders tightened. His neck muscles felt like steel cords. The connection between his past life and the relationship to Nina and Alex brought hot moisture to his eyes.

Fool. Jerk. Blockhead. He called himself every name he felt sure Nina wanted to call him. Just as he'd known he would, he'd made a mess of this, and now she and Alex were paying the price. If only there was a way to make it up to her...

Finding Alex unharmed: that was the only way.

"Clint?"

Her soft voice jolted Clint from his misery.

He coughed and blinked to clear his mind and vision. Still, his voice was gruff when he asked, "What?"

"Will you pray with me?"

"P-pray?" Shame washed over him again. Why hadn't he thought of that? Why hadn't it been his first response? He was less than useless, that's why. So arrogant that, even after his actions had chased the child away, he still thought that only his actions could save the day, when a much higher resource awaited them.

"Yes, Nina." He swallowed hard. "I'll pray with you. Do you want me to pull over or—"

"No, keep going. I think the Lord will understand if you don't close your eyes and bow your head this time." She reached across the truck's seat and placed her hand on his forearm, then bowed her own head. "Dear Lord, nothing is hidden from your eyes. Guide us now to find Alex, and keep your angels over him to shelter and protect him. Amen."

Clint paused, waiting. Finally, he asked, "That's it?"

"Is there something you want to add?"

He shook his head. Who was he to add a single word to a mother's heartfelt plea when he was responsible for her distress to begin with.

He had to get her to Alex. And Alex had to be all right. Period.

He drove on, swerving to avoid the deep ruts in the road. After what seemed an eternity, he pulled into the circular parking area where all the paths to the cabins met. The morning's sunshine had disappeared, and the sky was now gloomy with thick, billowing clouds building up around them.

Nina leaped from the truck, ducking her head against a barrage of dust and leaves kicked up by the wind.

"Nina, wait." In a few long strides, he overtook her as she dashed off down the path to the familiar cabin. "I'll go first."

"He's my son," she protested, grabbing at his shirt to pull him out of her way.

Clint relented and let her go ahead, his pace only a heartbeat behind hers.

"There it is," Nina said, pointing ahead the instant the chimney came into view. "Look, there's smoke coming out. That's a good sign, right?"

Clint said nothing. To him the notion of a young boy and fire did not seem a good sign at all. In fact, it made him want to hurry all the more, but he reined himself back to keep from trampling Nina on the narrow path and alarming her even more.

"It's just through here." She pushed aside a low tree limb to reveal the front of the cabin. Then she froze, and a piercing cry came from her lips, sounding as if it had been wrenched from her. "No!"

Clint heard her scream somewhere in the back of his mind even as his every instinct urged him past her, racing toward the smoke-filled cabin. His heart hammered in his ears. At the door, he pressed his palm against the surface to feel for heat; finding it cool, he pulled his collar up over his nose and mouth, then barged inside.

The stinging gray-black smoke brought a flood of tears to his eyes. "Alex? Alex, are you in here?"

"Alex?"

"Stay out of here, Nina. We can't afford to all get lost in this smoke."

"I want to find my baby," came her strangled cry.

"I'll do it, Nina. I will. Trust me. Just go back outside."

"I—"

"Go!"

Through the haze of smoke, he saw her figure stumble out the open door.

He saw her? In a real fire, he shouldn't be able to see his own hands, much less another person a few feet away. He waved his arm and cut a swath in the air through the pungent smoke. He neither saw nor heard any flames. Nor did he see or hear Alex. What he did see explained the smoke, though.

In two steps he had moved to the fireplace, and with one hard jerk, he pulled open the flue. The backdraft began to draw the smoke up and out of the cabin. Clint wiped his wrist over his brow and sighed. This could have been the work of a young boy, he decided, or a vagrant, or a lost hiker, or—had they made sure they'd doused the fire adequately before they left this morning? He couldn't remember.

Clint shook his head. The cabin looked just as they'd left it. No sign anywhere that Alex had been here.

"Nina?" he called out. "You can come in now."

"Did you find Alex?" she asked as she rushed inside, her expression filled with hope.

Squinting, Clint took one last look around the cabin and delivered the news. "No, Nina, he's not in the cabin. From what I can tell, he hasn't even been here."

Nina slumped against him and let his strength support her. She tried to make sense of his words, but she simply could not. "What do you mean, no sign? The fire—"

"Was probably caused by an old ember. We left in such a rush this morning I doubt if we doused the breakfast fire good enough."

Her knees wobbled. She tried to swallow but couldn't push past the hard lump in her throat. Her fingers slid over the smooth fabric of his shirtsleeve as she sank to the hearth. "What are we going to do now?"

He bent down to snag her under her arms and lift her to her feet again. "For starters, we aren't going to sit and worry. We don't have that kind of time."

"But if he's not here—"

"Just because he's not in the cabin doesn't mean he didn't head up here." Clint grasped her hand and started toward the back door. "We need to search all around this place."

"And what if we don't find him?" She slipped her hand from his but followed, her feet as heavy as lead.

"Then maybe we'll find a sign that will tell us where he is." Clint hurried ahead.

"A sign? As if that means anything," she said, her nostrils still filled with the odor of the fire.

Her sarcasm must have made a direct hit on Clint's nerves, she realized, watching as he came to a halt beside the door, his

208

back rigid. He placed his hands on his hips and turned his face to the ceiling.

"What kind of sign?" she pressed, wanting an explanation for his behavior more than an answer.

"How about this?" He lifted his boot, and the smell of fresh horse manure assaulted her nose. "That a good enough sign for you?"

"Plinkey," she murmured, her heart lightening at the prospect.

"You know another pony whose owner wants to drag him inside the house to weather a storm?"

She laughed. "I never guessed I'd be so happy to see something that disgusting, especially in the house."

"I'll bet the smoke scared 'em back outside." Clint threw open the door just in time to catch a slap of Plinkey's tail across his belly.

"Clint!"

"Alex?" Nina trod gingerly around the pony mess and poked her head out the door. "Alex, honey, are you all right?"

"Sure, Mama. God was looking after me—and Plinkey." He pulled on the pony's bridle and turned the animal around. "And I knew you'd come for me."

"Of course I'd come." Nina came around the Shetland and knelt in front of Alex, hugging him close.

When she released him, he said, "Not just you, Mama. I knew Clint would come, too."

"You did?" came a whisper from Clint.

Clint blinked and Nina noticed a misting in his eyes. She knew how much Alex's faith in him had touched the cowboy's rugged heart. If only she could do the same.

She looked up at the man she'd grown to trust and love. "I knew it, too, Clint. I knew when Alex was in trouble that you'd put our petty argument aside and help."

"If I hadn't got us into that argument in the first place—"

"Then you'd have gone on thinking you weren't the kind of man to be trusted by a family. And I'd have kept on thinking that I wasn't capable of running a business, of being a mother and a woman in love all at the same time—and still been too stubborn to admit that to do all those things, I'd need your help."

She suddenly realized he was staring at her with a dazed expression on his face. She frowned. "Clint?"

No response.

"Clint, are you listening to me?"

A slow smile spread across his lips and a teasing light came into his eyes.

She backed away a step, suddenly uncertain.

He moved forward a step, reaching out his hand to clasp hers. "Say that again."

"Say wh-what?"

"You were making a, let's say, confession."

She started to nip at a fingernail then stopped herself, tipping her chin up with a confidence she didn't feel. "I was saying I've been too stubborn to admit I need your help."

"Before that." He moved closer, and she felt her hip bump the treacherous monstrosity of a couch.

"Before?" She ran the words through her mind, knowing what she'd said but unable to voice them again until he'd given her something in return.

"You know what you said, Nina." He lowered his chin and his voice. "You called yourself a woman in love."

"I did?" She felt her cheeks redden under the intensity of his gaze. "I mean, yes, I did."

They stared at each other for a long moment. She wanted to scream at him to say something—anything—even if it broke her heart. Instead she whispered, "Don't you have something to say to me?"

"Yes, I do." He took her in his arms. "Nina Jackson?"

"Hmmm?"

"I love you."

Every one of her senses reeled with a rush of joy as he sealed his declaration with a kiss.

"Yippee!" Alex jumped in the air.

Still holding her close, Clint smiled down and chuckled. "And I'm pretty fond of your kid, too."

They both turned to Alex, and Clint held out his hand to bring the boy into their circle. He bent to scoop the child up, then straightened and turned.

"Ouch!" He flinched. "You two I love, but I'm not so sure about this pony."

Nina and Alex joined his laughter as they settled down to wait for the rest of the search party.

"Father, thank you for not forsaking a stupid fool like me. Thank you for binding my injuries, even though, through my own stubborn will, I tried to keep them always fresh by hiding them from your care, from the loving hearts of others, and even from myself. Thank you, Father, for your grace and for the giving hearts of Nina and Alex, who believe as it's written in Hosea that you will come to us, as surely as the sun rises. Thank you for the faith of a child, who trusted me and made me a father by faith, if not by birth. Amen."

"Amen," Nina echoed.

Clint placed his arm around her shoulder. They had stolen away for a few moments to give thanks for their many blessings and to talk about their future together. As they rejoined the staff and Mr. and Mrs. Jackson in the lobby, they found Alex regaling the delighted audience with the tale of the day's events.

"And then Clint steps in it!"

The crowd laughed.

Alex ducked his head and covered his mouth, his grin peeking from behind his fingers.

"So, that's how you knew it was Plinkey," Ellen surmised. "Because you knew he'd been in the house before."

Clint settled in an overstuffed chair, and Nina perched on the arm, her hand on his shoulder. "Funny how Plinkey has only gone in the house twice," Nina said, "and both times when it was getting ready to storm and Alex was around."

Clint threw a look of exaggerated panic at Alex. "Yeah, ha-ha, isn't that something?"

"You know what's also funny?" She leaned against him, cocking her head so that a strand of blonde hair brushed his temple.

Clint cleared his throat. "What's that, Nina?"

"How back in the cabin you said that Plinkey is the only pony you know whose owner drags him in the house during thunderstorms."

"Did I say that?"

"Yes, you did. And furthermore—"

"All right, Mama, I did it!" Alex threw up his hands. "I brought Plinkey inside the night Clint showed up. When you caught us, he was helping me take him back out."

"We didn't lie to you, Nina. But we did let you believe something that wasn't exactly the way it happened," Clint confessed.

"Or so you think."

"Huh?"

"Honestly, Clint. Did you really think I'd fall for a story about a Shetland pony who lets himself inside when it rains? Not to mention that Alex was ice-cold and wet that night." She poked him in the arm. "I may be a greenhorn, but give me some credit."

Clint sighed the most sincerely contented sigh he'd felt in more than five years. God had truly restored his life to him. That and much, much more.

"Does this mean we're not in trouble for that, Mama?" Alex asked from his seat on the floor.

"I think your punishment for running away—not being allowed to leave the ranch for two weeks, except for church—is enough for now, young man."

"What about Clint?"

"Hmm." She narrowed her beautiful eyes at him.

"She's not going to let me leave the ranch for a lot longer than that, son." He smiled at her. "'Course, I don't consider that a punishment."

"Are you saying you want to stay here permanently? To make this your home?" she asked softly.

"As long as I can do it as part of the family and not just as a business partner."

She pressed her lips together, her eyes glistening with unshed tears.

"Deal?" he asked in a hoarse whisper. He held out one hand with an uncertain look in his eyes.

She hesitated for the briefest of moments, then gently placed her hand in his. "Deal."

The group broke out with cheers and applause.

Nina saw the joy in Clint's eyes for the briefest of moments before she was pulled into his arms for a kiss.

Chapter
FOURTEEN

ere's comes the bride, big, fat, and wide. Here comes the groom, crazy as a loon!"

"Very clever." Nina gave Alex and Ellen a sly look, unable to keep a grin from bursting over her lips. "Too bad I didn't know we had such talent among us, or I'd have had you two sing at the wedding."

"I think they did fine as best man and maid of honor." Clint came up behind her to place his hands on her shoulders.

Ellen, still in her western-style bridesmaid's dress, waved her hand with a flourish to accept the compliment. Alex, apparently distracted before he'd finished changing clothes from the sunset wedding ceremony, stood in his dress shirt and a tattered pair of jeans.

All the wedding guests had departed except Ellen, who was manning the ranch's front desk, and Grammie and Paw-paw, who were staying to watch Alex while Nina and Clint honeymooned.

"Why don't you go on home now, Ellen. With the season over, it doesn't make sense for you to stay just to answer the phone." Nina pulled the thick shawl collar of her sweater closed.

"Oh, I don't mind. It's good practice for next year when you can afford to extend the season further into the fall." She smiled.

"Go home, Ellen, with pay." Clint dropped a kiss into Nina's hair. "It'll be our wedding gift to you."

"Actually—" Ellen ducked her head. "Mr. and Mrs. Jackson seemed so worn out from the trip out here and the excitement of the wedding, I told them I'd stay long enough to get Alex tucked in."

"Aren't you sweet?" Nina smiled.

"Well, it's the least I could do—being the head matchmaker and all." She shrugged.

"But really, it doesn't seem fair." Nina leaned back against her husband's broad chest. "You know my rule about the staff baby-sitting."

"What do you suggest we do?" Clint asked.

"Well, there's no law that says we have to go someplace for our wedding night." She lowered her lashes as she spoke. "You know I've said all along what a waste of money it is to go away on a honeymoon when we live in a place people come to for romantic getaways."

"And family vacations." Clint tilted his head toward Alex, reminding her how little privacy her plan would provide.

"Yes, but with the ranch having done so well this year and with our plans to expand and all, I just think the money we're laying out on a honeymoon might be better spent on something else."

"Such as?"

"Such as renovation of the mountain cabins."

"The—? Like a dog with a bone, that's you, Nina." He twisted her around so they faced one another. "You don't really think we can afford to waste our building capital refurbishing those raggedy old shacks, do you?"

"Better that than on ten days honeymooning in some exotic locale—the name of which you won't even tell me. What if I hate it?"

"You won't." He flicked his knuckle under her chin.

"What if I do?"

"Trust me, you won't." He looked into her eyes.

"Okay, but if I do hate it, will you promise me that we'll come straight home and get as much of our money back as possible?"

"Yes and no."

"What do you mean, yes and no?"

"Yes, we'll come home, but no, we won't be getting our money back—at least not until next season."

She blinked. "Run that by me again."

He laughed. "Yes, we'll come home. In fact, we'll already be home. But we won't get our money back, not until next season when we rent the place out for twice the cost of the ranch cabins."

"You didn't."

"Had the best cabin of the bunch fixed up and decorated just like you told me you wanted it."

"Oh, Clint!" She threw her arms around him.

"There's more." He hugged her tight. "I also had the old generator from this place fixed, and since it won't be used as much, it can power all five cabins until we can afford to get a better unit."

"I can't wait to see it."

"And I can't wait to carry you across the threshold." He kissed her despite the fact that they were both laughing. "Are you ready to go?"

"The suitcases you had Grammie pack for me are in the truck."

"Okay, then." He tugged on her arm, but she dragged her feet.

"Alex, honey, come give Mama a kiss bye-bye."

The boy planted a sweet kiss on her cheek, and then one on Clint's.

"And you behave for Ellen tonight and for Grammie and Paw-paw the rest of the time," she told him.

"I will, Mama." He gave her a smile so wide it looked as though his face might not be able to contain it. Nina returned the expression, then took Clint's arm, prepared to leave.

"Ellen, can I go to bed early tonight?" She heard her son say as they turned their backs.

"Why? Aren't you feeling well?" Ellen asked.

Clint and Nina paused, heads cocked, awaiting the child's answer.

"Oh, I'm okay."

Alex's assurance made them relax, and Clint reached out to open the door. Still, Nina's attention stayed on the conversation behind her.

"Just worn out from the wedding, kiddo?"

"Nope. I just can't wait to get to my good-night prayers."

"Why's that?"

"You know how last spring I prayed for God to give me and Mama a daddy?"

Nina couldn't help but feel wistful as she remembered, too.

"Yes," Ellen said.

"And Clint showed up and now he is my daddy?"

"Uh-huh."

Nina and Clint exchanged loving glances.

"Well, now that he and Mama are married, I need to say another prayer."

"To say thank you?"

"Yeah, that—"

Nina gave Clint's hand a squeeze.

"And something else."

They waited, framed in the doorway, the September breeze flowing fresh around them.

"Whatever he wants," Clint whispered in her ear, "I think we should consider trying very hard to see that he gets it."

"You've been his daddy six whole hours and already you're spoiling him," she teased in a hushed voice. "Besides, he's done a pretty good job with his prayers so far. Maybe we should just leave it in God's hands."

Clint nodded his agreement, then he and Nina leaned in to make sure they heard whatever sweet, childish whim the boy might have.

"Tonight when I say my prayers—" Alex's voice was soft but alive with excitement— "I'm going to ask God to send me a baby brother!"

Nina swallowed hard and cast a sidelong look at Clint, who grinned and ushered her out into the evening, closing the door firmly behind them.

Dear Reader,

My very first hero was my daddy. Strong and funny, sometimes harsh, he was a man of faith who truly loved his country and his family. I consider the love between him and my mother a true romance that created a model for me when I married. I am pleased to say that the Lord gave me a husband who is also a man of faith and a wonderful dad. That's why *Father by Faith* is such a special story for me, because I know firsthand how the love of a father can transform, shelter, and uplift a child.

I hope you had as much fun cheering on the often volatile romance between Nina and Clint as I did writing it, and that you enjoyed meeting the little boy, Alex, and his cantankerous Shetland pony, Plinkey.

Annie Jones

PALISADES...PURE ROMANCE

∼ PALISADES ∼

Reunion, Karen Ball
Refuge, Lisa Tawn Bergren
Torchlight, Lisa Tawn Bergren
Treasure, Lisa Tawn Bergren
Chosen, Lisa Tawn Bergren
Firestorm, Lisa Tawn Bergren
Surrender, Lynn Bulock
Wise Man's House, Melody Carlson
Arabian Winds, Linda Chaikin
Lions of the Desert, Linda Chaikin
Cherish, Constance Colson
Chase the Dream, Constance Colson
Angel Valley, Peggy Darty
Sundance, Peggy Darty
Moonglow, Peggy Darty
Promises, Peggy Darty
Love Song, Sharon Gillenwater
Antiques, Sharon Gillenwater
Song of the Highlands, Sharon Gillenwater
Texas Tender, Sharon Gillenwater
Secrets, Robin Jones Gunn
Whispers, Robin Jones Gunn
Echoes, Robin Jones Gunn
Sunsets, Robin Jones Gunn
Clouds, Robin Jones Gunn
Coming Home, Barbara Jean Hicks
Snow Swan, Barbara Jean Hicks
Irish Eyes, Annie Jones
Father by Faith, Annie Jones

Glory, Marilyn Kok
Sierra, Shari MacDonald
Forget-Me-Not, Shari MacDonald
Diamonds, Shari MacDonald
Stardust, Shari MacDonald
Westward, Amanda MacLean
Stonehaven, Amanda MacLean
Everlasting, Amanda MacLean
Promise Me the Dawn, Amanda MacLean
Kingdom Come, Amanda MacLean
Betrayed, Lorena McCourtney
Escape, Lorena McCourtney
Dear Silver, Lorena McCourtney
Enough! Gayle Roper
Voyage, Elaine Schulte

⌒ ANTHOLOGIES ⌒
A Christmas Joy, Darty, Gillenwater, MacLean
Mistletoe, Ball, Hicks, McCourtney
A Mother's Love, Bergren, Colson, MacLean
Silver Bells, Bergren, Chaikin, MacDonald (October, 1997)